REKI KAWAHARA ABEC bee-pee

SWORD ART ONLINE
Initial Ring V

026

SWORD ART ONLINE

§ **Alice**

An Integrity Knight of the Underworld and the world's first true bottom-up artificial intelligence.

§ **Asuna**

Kirito's girlfriend. She has the power of Stacia, Goddess of Creation, and is now referred to by the title of Star Queen.

"So...the rat can swim..."

§ **Stica**

Descendant of Tiese Schtrinen. At just twelve years old, she was cochampion of the Stellar Unification Combat Tournament with Laurannei.

"If they swim their hardest, they're even faster than fish."

§ **Airy**

The girl formerly in charge of the levitating platform in Central Cathedral. Has worked at the Dragoncraft Yard since the end of the War of the Underworld.

§ **Laurannei**

Descendant of Ronie Arabel and member of the Integrity Pilothood. Kirito and Asuna saved her when she was under attack from the Abyssal Horror.

"Kurrrrrr, kyurrr!"

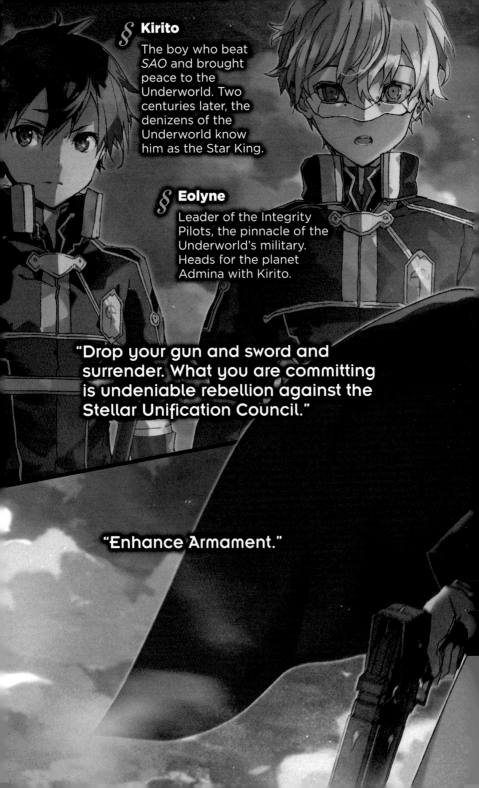

§ **Kirito**

The boy who beat *SAO* and brought peace to the Underworld. Two centuries later, the denizens of the Underworld know him as the Star King.

§ **Eolyne**

Leader of the Integrity Pilots, the pinnacle of the Underworld's military. Heads for the planet Admina with Kirito.

"Drop your gun and sword and surrender. What you are committing is undeniable rebellion against the Stellar Unification Council."

"Enhance Armament."

§ **Istar**

A mysterious figure called Your Excellency whose cold beauty hides an inner aura of dark, blazing flames.

⟪⟪ CHARACTERS

UNDERWORLD **UNITAL RING**

Kirito

The boy known as the Star King who brought the War of the Underworld to an end. In *Unital Ring*, he founded the town of Ruis na Ríg with his friends in the hopes of beating the game.

UNDERWORLD **UNITAL RING**

Asuna

Known as the Star Queen in the Underworld. In *Unital Ring*, she stands on the front line as a fencer, just as she did in *SAO*.

UNITAL RING

Kirito's Friends

Sinon

Fires a musket in *Unital Ring*. Her sub-weapon is the Bellatrix SL2.

Leafa

Kirito's sister. Does big damage up front with the Brawn ability tree and a bastard sword.

Yui

Kirito and Asuna's daughter. Fights as a player in *Unital Ring* with a dagger and fire magic.

Argo

A onetime info dealer in the *SAO* days. Makes use of her Swiftness to act as a scout.

Lisbeth

Blacksmith and mace-wielder. Kept her Blacksmithing skill from *ALO*, so she can make weapons and armor for her friends.

Silica

Uses short swords. Her skill at beast-taming means she can fight with Pina, the little dragon, and Misha, the thornspike cave bear.

Klein

Used a katana in *ALO*, but the skill he carried over was Pursuit. Now he uses a scimitar on the front line.

Agil

An ax-wielding merchant in *ALO*. He took the Toughness ability tree and acts as a tank.

Mocri

An *ALO* player. Tried to ambush Kirito but failed.

Hyme

Agil's wife. A player from *Insectsite*.

Friscoll

A scout for Mutasina's forces until Kirito's team captured him.

Other Players

UNDERWORLD **UNITAL RING**

Alice

The knight who helped Kirito bring peace to the Underworld. Now known as the Osmanthus Knight. Uses a bastard sword in *Unital Ring*.

Virtual Study Society

Mutasina

Leader of the Virtual Study Society. Sent an army of a hundred after Kirito with her Noose of the Accursed.

Viola

A swordswoman dressed in black. A member of the Virtual Study Society who is hostile to Kirito's group.

Dia

A member of the Virtual Study Society as well as Viola's identical twin. Powerful enough to rival Kirito and Asuna.

Magis

A dark mage wearing a black robe. Presumed to be the "Sensei" mentioned by Mocri's group.

Yzelma ——————— NPC

Leader of the Bashin living in Ruis na Ríg. A warrior who wields a burly scimitar.

THE UNDERWORLD

Eolyne Herlentz

The leader of the Integrity Pilots at just twenty years old. He has the same eyes and voice as Kirito's long-lost friend.

Laurannei Arabel

Ronie's descendant. Integrity Pilot and ace of the Blue Rose Company. She won the Stellar Unification Combat Tournament at just twelve years old.

Stica Schtrinen

Tiese's descendant and a fellow Blue Rose Company ace with Laurannei, whom she considers a close friend and rival.

Lagi Quint — Operator second class in the Integrity Pilots, Cattleya Company. Escorts Kirito to the space force base.

Orvas Herlentz — Present chairman of the Stellar Unification Council. Descendant of Bercouli, the first commander of the Integrity Knights. Eolyne's foster father.

Boharsson — Director of the North Centoria Imperial Guard. Attempted to interrogate Kirito for suspicion of using Incarnate weapons.

Phercy Arabel

Laurannei's younger brother and a student at North Centoria Primary Juvenile School. Anxious about his inability to activate ultimate techniques.

Selka Zuberg

Alice's younger sister. She is held on the eightieth floor of Central Cathedral in a state of deep freeze.

◀◀◀CHARACTERS

Shikimi Kamura
A new transfer to the returnee school. A member of the family that founded RCT's rivals, Kamura. She takes an interest in Asuna.

Tomo Hosaka (Argo)
Transferred to the returnee school at the same time as Shikimi. A writer and researcher for MMO Today.

Returnee School

Kazuto Kirigaya (Kirito)
Second-year high schooler and Asuna's boyfriend. Wants to attend Tohto Institute of Technology and eventually work for Rath.

Asuna Yuuki (Asuna)
Third-year high schooler and Kirito's girlfriend. A member of the elite. Her father is the former CEO of RCT, and her mother is a university professor.

Keiko Ayano (Silica)
A girl at the returnee school. Forms tight bonds with others through VRMMOs.

Rika Shinozaki (Lisbeth)
A third-year like Asuna. The moodmaker of the group.

Rath

Seijirou Kikuoka (Chrysheight)
Former SDF lieutenant colonel and a member of the Ministry of Internal Affairs and Communications' Virtual Divison. Spearheaded Project Alicization for Rath.

Rinko Koujiro
Rath's current director and a scientist who took part in the development of the Medicuboid. Was once Kayaba's lover.

Takeru Higa
Rath's chief technical engineer. Undertaking the refinement of Alice's machine body. Went to college with Kayaba and Rinko.

Others

Alice
A true bottom-up AI, in contrast to Yui, created through Project Alicization.

Suguha Kirigaya (Leafa)
Kazuto's sister, who picked up kendo in his stead and still practices it in her first year of high school. She's the vice-captain of the kendo team.

Shino Asada (Sinon)
A first-year at a different school. Kirito once saved her life.

Ryoutarou Tsuboi (Klein)
A worker at a small import company. A gamer friend from a different generation.

Andrew Gilbert Mills (Agil)
Owner of Dicey Café, a frequent hangout of Kazuto's friend group.

Akihiko Kayaba (Heathcliff)
Creator of *Sword Art Online*, the start of everything. Deceased.

SWORD ART ONLINE
unital ring V

VOLUME 26

Reki Kawahara

abec

bee-pee

YEN ON

NEW YORK

SWORD ART ONLINE, Volume 26: UNITAL RING V
REKI KAWAHARA

Translation by Stephen Paul
Cover art by abec

SWORD ART ONLINE Vol.26
©Reki Kawahara 2021
Edited by Dengeki Bunko
First published in Japan in 2021 by KADOKAWA CORPORATION, Tokyo.
English translation rights arranged with KADOKAWA CORPORATION, Tokyo,
through Tuttle-Mori Agency, Inc., Tokyo.

English translation © 2023 by Yen Press, LLC

Yen On
150 West 30th Street, 19th Floor
New York, NY 10001

Visit us at yenpress.com
facebook.com/yenpress
twitter.com/yenpress
yenpress.tumblr.com
instagram.com/yenpress

First Yen On Edition: March 2023
Edited by Thalia Sutton & Yen On Editorial: Payton Campbell
Designed by Yen Press Design: Andy Swist

Yen On is an imprint of Yen Press, LLC.
The Yen On name and logo are trademarks of Yen Press, LLC.

Library of Congress Cataloging-in-Publication Data
Names: Kawahara, Reki, author. | Abec, 1985– illustrator. | Paul, Stephen, translator.
Title: Sword art online / Reki Kawahara, abec ; translation, Stephen Paul.
Description: First Yen On edition. | New York, NY : Yen On, 2014–
Identifiers: LCCN 2014001175 | ISBN 9780316371247 (v. 1 : pbk.) |
   ISBN 9780316376815 (v. 2 : pbk.) | ISBN 9780316296427 (v. 3 : pbk.) |
   ISBN 9780316296434 (v. 4 : pbk.) | ISBN 9780316296441 (v. 5 : pbk.) |
   ISBN 9780316296458 (v. 6 : pbk.) | ISBN 9780316390408 (v. 7 : pbk.) |
   ISBN 9780316390415 (v. 8 : pbk.) | ISBN 9780316390422 (v. 9 : pbk.) |
   ISBN 9780316390439 (v. 10 : pbk.) | ISBN 9780316390446 (v. 11 : pbk.) |
   ISBN 9780316390453 (v. 12 : pbk.) | ISBN 9780316390460 (v. 13 : pbk.) |
   ISBN 9780316390484 (v. 14 : pbk.) | ISBN 9780316390491 (v. 15 : pbk.) |
   ISBN 9781975304188 (v. 16 : pbk.) | ISBN 9781975356972 (v. 17 : pbk.) |
   ISBN 9781975356996 (v. 18 : pbk.) | ISBN 9781975357016 (v. 19 : pbk.) |
   ISBN 9781975357030 (v. 20 : pbk.) | ISBN 9781975315955 (v. 21 : pbk.) |
   ISBN 9781975321741 (v. 22 : pbk.) | ISBN 9781975321765 (v. 23 : pbk.) |
   ISBN 9781975321789 (v. 24 : pbk.) | ISBN 9781975343408 (v. 25 : pbk.) |
   ISBN 9781975348960 (v. 26 : pbk.)
Subjects: CYAC: Science fiction. | BISAC: FICTION / Science Fiction / Adventure.
Classification: pz7.K1755Ain 2014 | DDC [Fic]—dc23
LC record available at https://lccn.loc.gov/2014001175

ISBNs: 978-1-9753-4896-0 (paperback)
      978-1-9753-4897-7 (ebook)

10 9 8 7 6 5 4 3 2 1

LSC-C

Printed in the United States of America

"THIS MIGHT BE A GAME, BUT IT'S NOT SOMETHING YOU PLAY."

—Akihiko Kayaba, *Sword Art Online* programmer

SWORD ART ONLINE
unital ring V

Reki Kawahara

abec

bee-pee

1

"……Selka!!"

Overcome with emotion, the Integrity Knight Alice Synthesis Thirty cried out and charged like a gust of wind.

The navy-blue hat atop her head couldn't withstand the force. It flew off, revealing long braids as she moved. I caught the hat in midair then sped after Alice.

My companions—Asuna, Integrity Pilot Commander Eolyne Herlentz, and his subordinates Laurannei Arabel and Stica Schtrinen—followed closely behind. In a matter of seconds, Alice had climbed the green slope in the middle of Central Cathedral's Cloudtop Garden and stopped just short of its peak.

On the flat top of the man-made hill was a single, aged broadleaf tree. It was not flowering at the moment, but my instinct told me it was an osmanthus tree.

Long, long in the past—only two years ago in my own time, but two centuries in the Underworld—Eugeo and I had come here to the eightieth floor and seen an osmanthus tree right in this spot. It hadn't been a real tree, however, but instead Alice's weapon, the Osmanthus Blade, transformed so it could absorb sacred power.

The sword was currently stuck in the unlocking mechanism for the great doors leading to the Cloudtop Garden. So the osmanthus tree ahead of us was presumably a real tree planted after the Otherworld War. But that wasn't the most important thing now...

"Selka," Alice said again, her voice barely audible this time. She stumbled uncertainly toward the shade under the tree.

Before her was a girl in a formal seated position, protected by the tree standing over her.

She wore a white veil and a vestment of the same color. Her closed eyelids and the hands resting on her lap were as white as alabaster. It was a cold texture that gave off no sense of vitality. But the details were too fine for her to be a statue, either. This was a real person who had been petrified—placed under the Deep Freeze art.

I knew her face and name. She had grown somewhat since the form I remembered, but there was no doubt that it was Alice's younger sister, Selka Zuberg.

Selka had been a nun in training in the tiny village of Rulid at the northern end of the realm. It was unclear how she had come to be petrified within Central Cathedral, but upon awakening from my two-month coma at the Rath office in Roppongi, I had apparently given a message to Alice, who was there waiting for me: *Alice, your sister, Selka, chose to go into deep freeze to wait for your return. She's still slumbering now, atop that hill on the eightieth floor of Central Cathedral.*

I had no memory of Selka being frozen here or of telling Alice about it, but those words had been the impetus for Alice, Asuna, and I to return to the Underworld. With the help of Eolyne and others, we had finally reached her.

Alice, dressed in the blue uniform of the Pilothood, knelt in front of the slumbering girl and placed her hands over her sister's. It did not have any magical dispelling effect.

"Selka...," Alice repeated, her voice tight. Asuna joined her and placed a hand on her trembling back. I wanted Selka to awaken as soon as humanly possible, but the art of Deep Freeze would surely require its own special art to undo it. I didn't know it, of course; the only ones who would have were the prime senator of the Axiom Church, Chudelkin, and Administrator...

I glanced around for clues and saw, about three feet away on either side, two other women standing watch over Selka.

Based on the texture, they seemed to have been frozen in the same way. Both wore robes that reached their feet, and their hands rested on the pommels of longswords, tips touching the ground. They were not wearing armor, but a familiar cross-and-circle insignia was stitched on the front flap of their robes, so they were surely knights. They seemed to be in their mid-twenties, if I had to guess...and then I noticed something else.

"Uh?" I gasped softly.

First, I stared closely at the woman on the right, then I examined the woman on the left before returning to the right again.

Their ages were nothing like I remembered them, but their faces, their general bearing...perhaps...

I spun around like I'd been struck, found the commander and the two pilots who were watching from an uneasy distance, and beckoned them to come closer.

"E-excuse me, Stica and Laurannei? Can you come over here?"

They seemed surprised by the summons, but promptly chirped, "Of course!"

Stica got up the slope first; I positioned her next to the woman on the left. Then I had Laurannei stand next to the knight on the right so I could compare the finer details.

They were very similar. If the girls aged another decade, they would probably look exactly like these two knights. Stica and Laurannei looked just like their ancestors from seven generations ago, too.

Which would mean these knights were...

"Are they...Ronie and Tiese...?" I murmured, stunned. The pilots were the first to react.

"What?!" "No way!!" they shrieked, spinning on their heels to examine the taller knights they were standing beside.

Alice and Asuna promptly turned away from Selka to see as

well. They initially looked up at me, then got to their feet, Alice staring at the knight on the left while Asuna peered at the one on the right.

After a few moments, Asuna pressed her hands to her mouth and whispered, "I-it really is Ronie. And this one is Tiese...But why are they...?"

I couldn't believe it, either. I had just assumed that after the Otherworld War, Ronie and Tiese had gotten married, had children, raised new knights, and after decades of happy life, had returned to the Lightcube Cluster from whence they'd come. At the very least, because of the existence of Laurannei and Stica, we knew they had children.

But nothing else was known. They could have given birth at a young age, then allowed themselves to be petrified while they were still young. But that would mean being permanently separated from their children while they were just babies; I couldn't imagine that such well-meaning girls would do something so cruel to their own families.

Was it not Ronie and Tiese's will to be frozen here? If so, what could have happened here two centuries ago...?

I was rooted to the spot, full of equal parts delight that their fluctlights were intact and confusion at the many questions they'd left behind. Alice approached me and grabbed my shoulder.

"Kirito, can you undo the petrification on Selka, Ronie, and Tiese with your Incarnation?"

"Wh-what...?!" I stammered, taken aback. But considering the possibility for a moment, I decided that it might actually work. However...

"I can't completely rule it out...but I'd prefer to undo the effect with the proper art. When I turned Amayori and Takiguri back into eggs, I just imagined time rewinding. But I can't fathom how you're intended to imagine turning people back to normal from the Deep Freeze effect. If I use Incarnation the wrong way or only partially undo the effect..."

Alice took her hand off my shoulder and clapped it over my mouth to stop me from talking.

"All right, you don't need to say any more...but I don't know the art to undo Deep Freeze, either...," she admitted dispiritedly, letting go of my mouth. She looked at the young pilot commander waiting behind us. "Eolyne, do you know?"

His answer did not surprise me.

"I'm sorry, but no. I've read about the Deep Freeze art, but nothing more than that...Today is the first time I have ever seen someone under its effect."

"...Ah. That's too bad...," she replied, looking away.

Asuna placed a comforting hand on her back again. "It's all right, Alice. Kirito told you that Selka was waiting for you here, didn't he? He wouldn't have said that if there wasn't a way to undo the petrification."

I wanted to back her up on that, but I had no recollection of that particular memory. If it was this Star King who had said that to Alice, shouldn't he have left behind a scroll or medicine or something that would undo the spell?

Stupid Star King, I grumbled to myself yet again. I approached Alice, too, and added, "Let's keep going for now. Maybe there's a tool or the art to undo the petrification farther up."

"......Yes. Maybe there is," Alice agreed weakly. She bent down to caress Selka's head once more, then looked past the osmanthus tree.

On the other side of the hill was another set of double doors identical to the ones behind us. The stairs to the eighty-first floor ought to be behind them, but my memories of that were faint, for some reason. It took a little thinking to understand why.

When Eugeo and I had navigated through the tower toward the top floor, where Administrator had lived, we'd fought against Alice here in the Cloudtop Garden. In no time at all, her powerful, flowing sword had me pinned to the wall. I'd activated my Perfect Weapon Control in a desperate attempt to turn the tables, but the force of it had gone haywire and blown a hole in the cathedral's wall, sucking me and Alice outside.

I'd kept a firm grip on her, despite her protests, and eventually convinced her to climb back up the wall with me and inside the tower again. Thinking back, our separation on the eightieth floor was the effective end of me and Eugeo's long journey together.

If I hadn't fallen out of the tower there...or if all three of us had fallen, maybe things would've turned out differently...

But I had to brush that intrusive thought away.

"Wait for me here," I stated. "I'll go get the swords from the unlocking device."

"Please, sir, allow us to handle an errand like that," insisted Stica, until I cut her off.

"Forcing a girl to carry such a damnably heavy object like that is a real-world taboo as serious as anything in the Taboo Index," I said, an awkward attempt at a joke. Stica and Laurannei looked surprised.

Asuna added, "It's also taboo to use the d-word to girls like that, Kirito."

"Oh. Pardon me," I said, hunching my shoulders guiltily.

I had just taken a step toward the downward slope of the hill when a heavy *clank!* rang across the enclosed garden.

It was the unlocking sound we'd heard when entering this place. But the huge doors ahead of me were still open. Which could only mean one thing.

I spun around as fast as humanly possible, just as Alice cried, "Kirito, the far doors!"

In moments I had sprinted back to the osmanthus tree, where I could see the south side of the garden past the trunk. At the bottom of the gentle slope, past the bridge over the little brook, the set of doors was slowly opening.

Technically it was only the left of the two doors, from our perspective. It didn't seem like there was a great host waiting behind it, but neither Asuna, Alice, nor I had our swords. In a pinch, I could probably use Incarnation to pull them out of the device and summon them back to our hands, but then it might get detected by the North Centoria Imperial Guard's Incarnameters.

If this looks like a dangerous foe, we'll flee at once, I told myself, watching the growing gap between the doors carefully.

At last, the door fell silent. It wasn't open all the way—barely a foot and a half, in fact. Stepping through into the garden, about as tall as Stica and Laurannei and around the same age, was a girl.

She had hair evenly cut above the shoulder, held back with clips shaped like bird feathers. Her dress was a gentle blue, covered with a brilliant white apron. There was a wicker basket in her hands. She carried no weapons.

The girl took a few plodding steps forward, at which point a brown shape came waddling after her. The long ears made me think it was a rabbit at first, but the body shape was more ratlike, and it measured about a foot long.

The girl and creature walked along the path and over the bridge. Where the path split in two directions, she ignored it and continued straight up the hill. A few seconds later, the bunny-mouse spotted us at the top, and it chirped, "*Skwirr!*"

She raised her head at the sound, looking quizzical at first, but her eyes gradually got wider as she realized what she was seeing.

Suddenly, she began racing up the hill. She lost her footing on the grass several times, slipping awkwardly. It made me want to shout, *You don't have to run!* but it didn't seem like the right situation for that. Fortunately, she made it to the top without falling. After taking a moment to catch her breath, she turned to the three of us under the tree.

At last, I realized that I recognized her.

She was the girl who had operated the levitating platform back in the days of Administrator. Was that really possible, though? When Eugeo and I had met her, she said she'd been doing the same job for 107 years already, and now it was another 200 years later. That would make her over 300 years old...twice the supposed time limit of the soul, which was estimated at 150 years. An incredible length of time.

"Ummm…are you…?"

…*really that platform operator?* I wanted to ask.

But as if to answer that unspoken question, the girl's deep-blue eyes opened wide, and she spoke in a flat voice that was exactly as I remembered it.

"Lord Kirito…Lady Asuna…Lady Alice."

Trembling droplets gathered at the corners of her eyes and then fell onto her apron.

But that was the extent of her outward show of emotion. She set down the basket, folded her hands against her lap, and bowed deeply.

"Welcome back."

Her quiet, tremulous voice was accompanied by the squeak of the bunnymouse. "*Skwirrk!*"

2

The little brown creature was a long-eared wetrat, and she called it Natsu.

Natsu was now resting on Laurannei's lap, happily gnawing on something that looked like a walnut. We were sitting in a circle on a blanket the platform operator had brought out, and the creature examined the entire group of us before settling on Laurannei. Had it been totally at random, or was there a method behind its choice? I could only wonder about the answer as I sipped my cofil tea.

Mysteriously, not only did the platform operator's basket contain a picnic blanket large enough to seat ten people, she also had eight cups in there. It was as if she'd come prepared, knowing we were all going to visit today. But if so, why had she welled up with tears when she saw me, Asuna, and Alice?

I had so many questions, but after pouring the cofil for us, the platform operator got up and walked over to Selka, Ronie, and Tiese. She used a large brush with strangely colored bristles to carefully sweep the dust off the three statuesque figures.

As a matter of fact, two hundred years spent under a tree would lead to a lot more than just a little pile of dust. The fact that the girls weren't covered in vines and moss was presumably because the platform operator came by regularly to clean them...But even still, this was two centuries we were talking about.

"I...," murmured Asuna, cradling her cup of tea and watching the operator work quietly and diligently, "I only remember saying hello to her a few times, but for some reason, she feels so familiar to me."

She looked over at Natsu, who was stretched out faceup on Laurannei's legs, and reached out to scratch the creature's fluffy neck.

"Same with this one..."

I was feeling the exact same thing as Asuna. In fact, I was starting to feel like the platform operator was supposed to have another name.

"...You know her, don't you, Alice?" I asked.

The knight nodded. "Yes, when I lived in the cathedral, I rode on her platform once every few days at least and sometimes gave her treats for her trouble. But...she seems a bit different from the operator I remember."

"Hmm...and you, Eolyne?" I asked. The pilot commander, who had been sitting politely across from me, suddenly lifted his head in surprise. Behind the white leather mask that covered the upper half of his face, his green eyes blinked rapidly.

"Sorry...I wasn't listening."

"Oh, no, I'm sorry for throwing it to you out of nowhere. Did you know about her, too, Eolyne?"

"Er, no, of course not," he said, shaking his head, then took his commander's hat off and rested it on his knees. His wavy flaxen hair shone in the sunlight coming through the windows high on the wall. "I didn't even know that anyone was living in the sealed floors of Central Cathedral. How is she getting food and water up here...?"

"That's a good question..."

Even if she had a major stockpile of supplies, the water and food ingredients would reach the end of their life within the span of two centuries. But out of all the questions and concerns in my head, that one was not very high on the list.

I kept nursing my cofil to keep my impatience at bay, and after ten minutes, the operator returned from her task and knelt formally on the blanket.

"Would anyone like to freshen up their cofil?" she asked.

I was going to decline, but Stica raised her hand first.

"Oh, I'll have some! This cofil is really, really delicious!"

"C'mon, Sti, don't be presumptuous," scolded Laurannei, much to Stica's glee.

"Oh, sure, Laura, but the first thing you did after you took a sip was make that *Oooh, nummy!* face."

"Wha…?! I don't talk like that!"

For one fleeting moment, I thought I detected the faintest hint of a smile crossing the platform operator's lips. But it was gone just as quickly. In her calm, reserved manner, she stated, "This cofil is known as Moonlit Evening. It was developed by the Star Queen. As far as I am aware, it is not grown anywhere in the Underworld except for this very place."

"Meaning, in the Cloudtop Garden?" Stica asked, looking around.

The operator shook her head. "No, on the ninety-fifth floor."

"…The Morning Star Lookout…"

It was Alice. I recalled that name as well. It was the one place in the hundred-floor Central Cathedral where the walls were open to the outside. If not for that place, Alice and I would not have been able to get back inside the tower after we fell from this floor.

More than the ninety-fifth floor, however, I was curious about the mention of the Star Queen's strain of tea leaves. I glanced at Asuna, who didn't seem to be skeptical about this information at all. She took another sip of cofil and beamed at the operator.

"It's really very good. And I love the name: Moonlit Evening."

"…The Star Queen said she took the name from a tanka she read in the real world a very long time ago."

I was just marveling at how natural the word *tanka* sounded, coming out of her mouth, when Asuna said, "I had a feeling that was the case. See, Kirito?"

"S-see what?"

"I think we have to admit that it's true."

"Wh-what's true?"

"That I'm the Star Queen, and you're the Star King."

"......"

I was surprised to see that Eolyne, Stica, Laurannei, and even Alice and the operator were staring at me keenly. The only one present who wasn't curious about my reaction was Natsu, who was soundly sleeping on Laurannei's lap.

"...And, um, what part of this conversation made you think of that...?" I pressed.

Asuna stretched and quoted the poem: "Like a shadow cast by the first rays of the morning sun after a moonlit evening, I am rendered insubstantial by the thought of you."

She received a round of applause with some measure of bashfulness.

"That's a tanka poem from the eleventh book of the *Man'yoshu*, but the writer is unknown, and it's not one of the more famous poems. I really like it, though, and I've always had it memorized for some reason."

"So you're saying...it's extremely unlikely that anyone *other* than you would choose a term from that poem to name their strain of cofil tea?"

Asuna's head bobbed. I surveyed the other faces staring in our direction, then said, "Fine. I'll admit it, then. I guess the Star King who ruled the Underworld up until thirty years ago *was* me, after all."

Immediately, Stica and Laurannei broke into huge, excited smiles. Eolyne just shrugged, as if to say, Now *he admits it*.

"But let me be clear...Just because I'm acknowledging it doesn't mean Asuna and I remember it. So, um..." I looked to the platform operator and asked her, "Sorry...you had another name, right?"

She straightened up, seemingly prepared for this very question, and said, "Yes. My name is Airy."

Eolyne's shoulders twitched, I thought. But he said nothing, so I glanced at the girl again and repeated, "Airy..."

Despite having never heard it before, it just felt *right*, as though she couldn't have had any other name. I repeated it once more in my head, then asked, "Why are you here? Why aren't you frozen the same way these three are…?"

"Because I wished for it to be that way," Airy said without missing a beat. She took a sip of cofil and then began to tell her story.

It was the year 441 when the second commander of the Human Unification Council's sacred artificers brigade, Selka Zuberg, as well as the Integrity Knights Tiese Schtrinen Thirty-Two and Ronie Arabel Thirty-Three were put to rest here…sixty years after the creation of the Unification Council.

That was the year the traditional Integrity Knighthood was disbanded and replaced by the new Integrity Pilothood. The knights were allowed to choose between transferring to the new order, quitting to live their lives freely, or undergoing the Deep Freeze art.

But it was not a knight who first requested to be petrified. It was Lady Selka, the commander of the sacred artificers brigade. It was the original commander, Ayuha Furia, who took decades to analyze and decipher the lost art of Deep Freeze. Lady Selka took over that work, and Lady Tiese's children were fully grown by then; they said that Lady Selka would be lonely on her own, and joined her in her deep sleep.

Some of the knights chose to transfer, and some chose to start a new life, but many of them wished to be frozen, too. After some time had passed, in the year 475, Lady Fanatio, the longest-serving at the royal side, entered eternal slumber…and three years after that, the Royal Highnesses entrusted all their authority to the Human Unification Council and retired from the throne.

I believe even you pilots know what happened next. In the year 480, the Human Unification Council was renamed the Stellar Unification Council, and the Human Era calendar was renamed the Stellar Era calendar. That same year, everything from the eightieth floor of Central Cathedral and up was sealed, so no one could enter aside from the king and queen, and myself and Natsu.

From that point on, the Star King and Queen led a very relaxed and dignified life, but they, too, went to their eternal rest. I witnessed them disappear after being engulfed in light in Stellar Year 550. As they instructed me, I informed the Stellar Unification Council that they had left the Underworld, and I passed on the message that His Highness left behind. I have minded this place in the thirty years since, keeping it ready for the moment my masters returned.

"...Lady Alice, Lady Asuna, Lord Kirito. I say again...welcome back."

With her long, long explanation concluded, Airy placed her hands atop her lap and bowed deeply.

Asuna shot to her feet without warning. She made her way around the cofil pot and kettle stand in the middle of the blanket, then went down on a knee before Airy, thrust her hands out, and clutched the girl's thin body against her own.

"I'm sorry...I'm so sorry, Airy. You must have been so lonely, all by yourself...for thirty years..."

It was all I could do to stifle the urge to repeat Asuna's action. Inwardly, I cursed the Star King, my former self, for putting Airy through this cruel, solitary ordeal.

But just as quickly, Airy replied, "No, Lady Asuna. As I said a moment earlier...all of this was by my own insistence." She placed her hands gently on Asuna's shoulders. "They instructed me to sleep anywhere in the cathedral I desired, but I would not be able to respond to unforeseen events that way, and most importantly, there would be no one left to welcome back all three of you if you should return."

"Welcome us...?" Asuna repeated indignantly. Airy gently pushed her shoulders back.

"Lady Asuna, I was blissfully happy to have served you and Lord Kirito. You made my dreams come true...so of course I would remain here to wait while you were gone. I was not lonely. I had Natsu to keep me company, thanks to Lady Ronie."

The moment she said its name, Natsu perked its head up from Laurannei's lap and cried, *"Kyrrr!"*

The girls giggled at the way the rodent seemed to be confirming her statement. Asuna was feeling calmer, too, and with a gentle nod, she let go of her grasp around the other girl's back. She didn't return to me, however, but sat down at Airy's side.

Just as things were feeling relaxed and casual again, Eolyne broke his silence with a nervous question. "If you'll pardon my asking...are you the original yardmaster of the Integrity Pilothood's Dragoncraft Yard One, Airy Trume...?"

It took me a few moments to realize what "dragoncraft yard" meant. It was most likely the factory where they constructed the fighter jets that Laurannei and Stica flew. And Airy was the original yardmaster? Was Trume her last name?

Another thought occurred to me: Airy had traded words with Eugeo two centuries ago. Eolyne was wearing a mask, but he had an almost identical face, hair, and voice. It was strange that, unlike Alice, she had no reaction to him at all.

I waited with bated breath for her response. Airy grinned faintly and replied, "There was a time when I held that role...but all I did was tell everyone at the yard the things I learned from my master. Please just call me Airy."

"I could never...If it were not for you, Lady Trume, my grandfather told me that it would have taken another thirty years to develop and deploy mass-produced crafts," Eolyne insisted.

She blinked slowly, as though seeing the distant past against the back of her eyelids, and said simply, "It was very, very long ago."

I was curious what she felt, talking to Eolyne, and I was also curious about Eolyne's grandfather—the father of Orvas Herlentz, chairman of the Stellar Unification Council—but the day would be over before I finished asking every last question that came to mind. The Underworld was not under any kind of time acceleration at the moment, so every tick of the second hand here was also a second passing in the real world.

Over there, it was Saturday, October 3rd, so there was no school, but Dr. Rinko Koujiro from Rath had instructed us to log out by five o'clock at the very latest. The eleven-thirty bells had just rung earlier, so we had another five and a half hours of time to go. Could we travel to Admina as Eolyne had requested and find the person who tried to kill Stica and Laurannei in that span of time?

At any rate, we'd learned the reason that Selka, Ronie, and Tiese were frozen here, and that Airy was taking care of them, so I decided it was time to move on from the topic.

"Um, Airy...I want to thank you for carrying out this very important job. It's very frustrating that I have no memory of being the Star King, and I feel bad about it, but all the same, I'm very happy to see you again."

"I am, too, my lord," she said, smiling furtively. I sidled a few inches closer along the ground to reveal the reason we were here.

"Now, as you may have figured out already...we're back in the Underworld to help awaken Alice's sister, Selka. And Tiese and Ronie, of course. Do you know how to do that?"

"I do," Airy said. Alice promptly exhaled with relief, then collected herself and looked stern again.

"Miss Airy, what is this method? Is it a sacred art...?"

"Yes. However...as much as it pains me to tell you, the entirety of the Deep Freeze art that Lady Ayuha and Lady Selka restored remains strictly sealed and kept somewhere else."

"Somewhere else, meaning outside the cathedral...somewhere in Centoria?"

"No. It is not in the human realm or the dark realm or on the outer continent, even. The sealed chest is hidden on the planet Admina."

3

We helped Airy gather up the blanket and teaware, said good-bye to the frozen women for now, and headed higher up in the cathedral.

Of course, we retrieved our four swords from the locking mechanism, too, but when I pulled them out, the large doors began to close again, and I had to hurry back into the garden before they shut. A little push did not budge them in the slightest; we'd just have to trust that Airy could open them for us from the inside.

The doors on the south side were unlocked and gave way to a familiar staircase covered in red carpet. Eugeo must have taken these stairs on his own back then. Airy guided us upward until Alice stopped, just before we reached the ninetieth floor.

"Miss Airy...what happened to the bath that was on this floor?" she asked.

Memory flooded back into me: Yes, on the ninetieth floor of Central Cathedral, there was an enormous bath that took up the entire floor. But the doors on the other side of the landing were closed, so there was no way to know what was behind them.

"It still exists, Lady Alice," Airy said matter-of-factly. "The pontifex's art upon the Great Bath is still active, so even now, centuries later, its hot water is clean and pure. But the Star King renovated the interior so that it is separated into a women's area and a men's area. There was also an entrance directly to the bath from the levitating platform shaft on the north end, but it is currently sealed off."

"Huh? A bath?!" "There's a bath all the way up here?!" exclaimed Stica and Laurannei.

With no small amount of pride, Asuna explained, "It's incredible. The bath is so big you can swim back and forth in it, and all the walls are windows, so not only can you see all of Centoria, you can also even see all the way to the End Mountains when the weather is clear."

"You remember the baths, Asuna?" I asked without thinking.

Annoyed, the former Star Queen snapped, "Of course I do. After the Otherworld War, when we came back to the cathedral with Ronie and Tiese, I took two baths a day. You always said, 'Later, later,' so maybe you don't remember that."

"Ohhh..."

Upon reflection, that sounded familiar. But at the time, I was so busy with Fanatio and Deusolbert attempting to forge peace with the Dark Territory that I didn't have the time to sit in a bath and soak.

I had always assumed that all of the Integrity Knights I'd fought the Otherworld War alongside—if you ignored the fact that I was in a coma right up until the final battle—were dead by now. But if Airy was correct and many knights had chosen the deep freeze, then I might be able to see some of them again, as long as we got the sacred art to unfreeze them.

The problem, however, would be the life span of the soul, as the sage Cardinal once explained to me. If that was one of the reasons the knights chose sleep, I couldn't just go waking them up on a whim. It was a mystery how Airy could still be alive (or so it seemed) long after she'd crossed that time limit, but I didn't think I wanted to ask her about that to her face.

I was staring dully at the door to the bath, lost in thought, when Alice approached on my right and said, "Kirito, I understand

that you want to use the bath, but we don't have time for that right now."

And from the left, Asuna said, "That's right, Kirito. We need to go to Admina and get that sealed chest. We can worry about the bath after that."

"R-right. Let's keep moving," I replied.

Of course, on the inside, I was muttering, *You two are the ones who actually want to go in there...*

Another five floors up the staircase later, we walked headlong into a flood of bright light.

Natsu squealed and leaped out of Laurannei's arms, hopping nimbly up the steps that were nearly half its height. We trotted after it.

Unlike the landings that appeared at each of the previous floors, this was an open space with railings on three sides. When I reached the floor after Natsu and the two pilots, I initially squinted at the light, but when I realized what I was looking at, I gaped.

The ninety-fifth floor of Central Cathedral was the Morning Star Lookout.

Two hundred years ago, Alice and I worked together to climb the tower's outer wall, only barely making it up to this place with our lives. The outer rim of the floor had previously been open to the air, but now there were trees of all kinds planted along it, serving as a kind of blind to the outside.

What the trees were hiding was an all-white airplane resting in the center of the floor.

A dragoncraft.

"W-wowwww!" Stica exclaimed. The others were speechless when they caught up.

The pilots saw dragoncraft just about every day, so their shock could only come from the size of this one. Its length spanned half the floor, over eighty feet. The girls' dragoncraft were about fifty feet, as I recalled, so it was significantly larger.

And unlike the Integrity Pilots' dragoncraft, whose bodies were simple exposed steel, this was made of a pure-white material with a touch of translucence. A long vertical canopy was in the same color, and the wings were quite short in comparison to the length of the body. There were three heat-element exhaust ports, on the tail and under the base of each wing.

Despite its massive size, it didn't seem ponderous thanks to its flowing design. This struck me as an aircraft that had been designed with no combat capability in mind, focusing solely on long-distance flight.

I stepped backward until I was next to Eolyne, and murmured, "Is this...the Star King's dragoncraft? The one you talked about?"

"...I can guarantee it, even though I've never seen it for myself. Just look at that," said the pilot commander, pointing out the right side of the hull, just under the canopy. I squinted and saw it was inlaid with silver alphabet letters—or *sacred script*, as they called it here. It read X'RPHAN XIII. It was a strange sequence of letters, but I knew right away that it was pronounced *Zurfan*. It was spelled exactly like the name of the white dragon that was a field boss on the fifty-fifth floor of Aincrad.

"So that's the thirteenth X'rphan, huh...?" I murmured.

Airy turned back and nodded to me. "Yes, the final dragoncraft that the Star King created. He rolled it out a hundred years ago, but it's still in perfect condition."

"Were you maintaining it, too, Airy...?"

"That's right. But it's nothing more than the occasional washing of the surface with water elements and giving the eternal-heat and wind elements in the sealed canisters a little rev to freshen them up."

"But...goodness, you've done so much for us...How can I even begin to thank you?" I said, at a loss to describe my gratitude. She'd been so considerate, so faithful.

"Look over there," she said, pointing at a strange object in the corner, far away from the dragoncraft.

It was a metal disc about five feet across. The thickness was less than four inches on its own, except for the pair of tubes attached to the underside like tanks. A number of small nozzles were lined up along the outer edge. Several handrails were attached all around the top of the disc so that people could ride on it, but it was totally unclear what kind of tool it was meant to be...

Suddenly, deep in my head, I thought I heard the voice of my long-lost friend.

If the Church disappears, and you're released from this calling, what would you do...?

And in response, the voice of Airy—the platform operator.

If I had a wish...I wish that I could fly this platform out there... wherever I could go...

"Is that...a levitating platform...capable of free flight through the sky...?" I asked.

Airy's head bobbed deeply. "It is. I call it a flying platform. Because it has no wings, it required countless rounds of experiments and improvements until it was able to fly in a stable fashion, but Lord Kirito never gave up. He said it was a promise he and Lord Eugeo made with me..."

"......I see."

Even I knew it was a weak, curt reply, but I couldn't think of anything to add. If I'd tried, I wouldn't have been able to hold back the tears.

Inside my head, I was about to pay a major compliment to the persistence of the Star King, whom I still couldn't believe was myself—but then I realized at last that Airy had just mentioned the name of my friend, which I had been unable to say in the presence of Eolyne Herlentz.

I held my breath and glanced to the right.

A moment later, Eolyne looked at me. Behind the glass lenses embedded in the mask, I could see his eyes blinking rapidly.

"...What's the matter, Kirito?" he asked. His voice seemed just a bit more enigmatic than usual—but it also sounded no different than before. His expression seemed as calm as ever, but he also looked a bit disoriented to me.

If I'd been observing his expression the entire time, I might have been able to detect a change in his manner at the moment he heard Eugeo's name, but it was too late to find out now. Even still, I didn't have the courage to intentionally drop that name in conversation again.

"No...it's nothing," I said, shaking my head. I turned to Airy. "When you mentioned making your dream come true down on the eightieth floor, you were talking about this flying platform?"

"That is correct, but it is not the only thing," she replied, bringing her right hand to the chest of her apron. "I used to think that operating the levitating platform was my entire reason for being alive, but you and Lady Asuna...and the Integrity Knights, and the Unification Council, and Master Sadore...You all taught me about joy, pleasure, sadness, and loneliness. The majority of my memories and feelings have been compressed, so it takes time to remember...but they are always a warmth in my chest. It meant that I never found my wait here to be painful."

She smiled again, and I nodded slowly. "I see...Well, that makes sense..."

Before I realized what I was doing, I lifted my hand to press right over my heart.

The memories are here. Here for all eternity.

I repeated these words, etching them into my being, and looked around the ninety-fifth floor once again.

The trees that hid this floor from view completely filled every side of the space. There was absolutely no way for anyone to see the space from the outside—not that there was a single building in Centoria even close to being this high up. But it also made it feel as though there was no exit for the dragoncraft.

"Ummm, Airy...in order to send the dragoncraft off, do we need to cut down these trees?" I asked. The former platform operator almost rolled her eyes.

"That will not be necessary. The trees are in planters that can be moved."

"Oh. Okay. That makes sense." That left just two doubts in my mind: "And the dragoncraft can fly to the planet Admina?"

"Of course."

"How many can ride in it?"

"It seats two."

"......Uh-huh."

I took another look at the lineup around me. Pilot Commander Eolyne Herlentz asked me to travel to Admina and investigate what was happening there. That meant one of the two in the dragoncraft had to be Eolyne, with me being the other, I assumed. Asuna and Alice would just have to wait here, however many hours the investigation took.

Before I could open my mouth to speak, Laurannei announced, "Commander Eolyne, we will accompany you in our craft!"

Stica added, "We cannot allow you to undergo the danger of an unofficial investigation in Admina without any kind of personal detail!"

"Wh-what...?" stammered the commander, taken aback. He lifted his hands. "Remember, we went to the trouble of coming all this way because we can't use the Pilothood's dragoncraft..."

"We can always come up with a reason! Battle training, testing new equipment, and so on!" Laurannei persisted. While her features were identical to her distant ancestor's, her personality was a little—no, *more* than a little fiery in comparison to Ronie's.

According to Airy's earlier explanation, Ronie and Tiese gave birth at a young age, raised their children well, and went into petrification when they were close to eighty years old. But in the Cloudtop Garden, they looked no older than their mid-twenties to me. That would mean they'd undergone some kind of life-freezing art around that age, but like the Deep Freeze sacred art, that was a secret only Administrator was supposed to have known.

Meanwhile, the girls were still hounding Eolyne about his decision.

"Lady Stica, Lady Laurannei," interrupted Airy, who seemed almost as though she were enjoying herself the tiniest bit, "I'm afraid that outside of the atmosphere, the standard issue Keynis Mk. 7 dragoncraft the Integrity Pilothood uses can travel only half as fast as the X'rphan Mk. 13. If you are to escort them, Lords Kirito and Eolyne will have to spend much longer traveling."

"Half?!" the two girls said at the exact same moment.

I was just as shocked. I'd thought that special experimental units and one-offs that had better specs than a standard model were something that happened only in anime and video games, but the Star King had rather immaturely overturned that assumption. The stark difference in specs cowed the pilots into acceptance, and they did not argue any further.

Relieved, I approached Asuna and Alice and murmured, "So based on what you just heard, me and Eolyne will go to Admina and…"

I stopped and took a half step away when I saw the way they were glaring at me.

"Remember, Kirito, 'Strange Fish Shout, Run, and Report.'"

"Um…wh-what was that again?" I asked, furrowing my brow.

Fortunately, Alice could recite the whole saying. "Don't follow any Strangers, don't get into any Fishy cars, and be sure to Shout. Run away at the first sign of danger, and Report back with what happens."

What am I, a little kid?! I wanted to shout, but I had too much self-control for that. Instead, I replied, "G-got it. I'll be careful. I think you're probably safe here, but just in case…"

"Nothing to worry about," said Alice flatly. She stepped forward and grabbed my hand. "I'm serious, though, Kirito. We must have the sealed chest that contains the formula to the Deep Freeze art."

"I know. I swear I'll get it back," I promised, clapping her hand with my own and giving Asuna a nod.

Eolyne and the pilots had just finished their own private conversation. I gazed up at the massive dragoncraft occupying the center of the floor and thought, *Help us, X'rphan. If I'm going to help Alice and Selka reunite, and bring Ronie and Tiese back, I need your power.*

The craft was in perfect condition, so it took only ten minutes to be ready to leave.

Eolyne, now dressed in his pilot's uniform, took the front seat while I sat in the back. Once the canopy was down and I'd attached my seat belt, I gave the OK sign, so Airy pressed a hidden button near the stairs.

The trees in their massive marble planters directly ahead of us began to slide left and right out of the way. In no more than ten seconds, there was an open space more than wide enough for the craft to slip through, with nothing but blue sky ahead.

"All right, Kirito, here we go."

"Whenever you're ready," I replied. A high-pitched vibration emitted from the rear of the craft. I had been questioning how we were going to take off without a runway of any kind, but this cleared it up: The X'rphan Mk. 13 had the ability to do a vertical ascent. The massive body lifted about a foot and a half off the ground, then slid forward through the air.

"Activating deception device," Eolyne announced, flipping a toggle switch on the instrument board. This time the craft made a crackling sound. The parts of the white body I could see through the canopy material were turning transparent somehow. Now the people of Centoria wouldn't see the X'rphan craft even if they happened to be looking up into the sky.

I swiveled around one last time to see Airy, Natsu, Stica, Laurannei, Alice, and Asuna standing before the stairs. The two pilots saluted, Alice gave a familiar old knight's greeting, and Airy and Asuna waved.

My response was a big thumbs-up. I whispered to my pilot, "Hey, Eolyne, may I say the words?"

"Huh? What words?"

"These ones," I said, clearing my throat. "X'rphan Mk. 13, takeoff!!"

A bit later, the vibration got just the tiniest bit louder. Instead of the *booom skreeee* roar I expected, the massive dragoncraft slid forward smoothly and politely, as powerful and genteel as a luxury car.

About fifty feet away from the tower, the craft began to rise while maintaining a level position. Centoria got smaller and smaller below, until I could see the farms and pastures surrounding the city.

Once our ascent speed reached a stable rate, Eolyne said apologetically, "I hate to disappoint after your very lively command, but this is about all we can manage until we reach an elevation of three thousand mels. When the main propulsion goes at full speed, it makes a hell of a sound."

"Oh, I see. How long does it take to reach three thousand mels?"

"About ten minutes."

"Hmmm…and how long to Admina?" I asked.

The commander's blue helmet tilted to the right. "Well…if Miss Airy is correct that the X'rphan Mk. 13 is twice as fast as a Keynis Mk. 7, the entire flight should take about an hour and a half, I guess…"

"An hour and a half," I repeated, frowning heavily.

At the mansion near the base, Eolyne had said it was a six-hour trip from Cardina to Admina on one of the big passenger craft. That would mean the standard fighting Keynis could do it in three hours, and the one-off unique X'rphan craft at half that again. It seemed to make sense.

But even six hours seemed like it was too fast. In the real world, the Mars probes that different countries were shooting over on giant rockets took about eight months to reach the planet. Of course, the Underworld probably wasn't created on the same scale as the real solar system, but if the trip could be done in six hours, it seemed like it should be closer than Earth and the moon in real life. If there was another planet of the same size that close, it should be big enough to completely blot out the night sky with its presence.

"Um...Eolyne?"

"What?"

"I know it's a bit late to ask this, but how many kilome—er, how many kilors apart are Cardina and Admina?"

"About five hundred thousand kilors, I think."

"Five hundred thousand..."

That was farther away than the moon from Earth, but over a hundred times closer than Mars at its closest.

"Um, i-in that case, shouldn't Admina be clearly visible from Cardina?"

"Huh? Of course it's visible," Eolyne said, more exasperated than I'd ever heard him before. He leaned his head back. "In fact, at this time of day..."

He was gazing through the clear canopy of the cockpit, then pointed straight forward.

"There. Right there."

I craned my neck to follow Eolyne's finger and saw a whitish star floating near the horizon. I blinked, then straightened in my seat. "Um, but that's the moon...Lunaria, right?"

"That's the old name."

"Huh...?"

Stunned, I tried to grab the back of the seat in front of me and lean forward, but my seat belt held me in place. So instead I jutted my head forward as far as I could and shouted, "Wait a second! Admina is Lunaria?! So when you traveled there, it turned out not to be a tiny satellite, but a huge planet?!"

"Well, it's still on the smaller side. The diameter of Admina is only about half of Cardina's. So Cardina is the primary planet, and Admina is the secondary."

"N-no kidding..."

"By the way, His Majesty the Star King was the first person to reach Lunaria in a dragoncraft."

"No kidding," I repeated, and gazed again at the moon—no, planet—hovering in the sky. True, the size seemed about twice as big as the moon did when seen from Earth, but to think that it wasn't just a satellite...But then another thought occurred to me.

"But wait a second. The sigil of the Stellar Unification Council that we saw on the first floor...Isn't the big circle in the middle supposed to be Solus, with the dot in the upper right being Cardina and the dot in the lower left as Admina? If the two planets are supposed to be rotating around Solus on opposite sides of the sun, then Admina shouldn't be visible from here, right...?" I asked, gesturing to demonstrate my point.

"That's just an artistic touch," he said simply. "In fact, Admina and Cardina are lined up very closely on their respective orbits. Cardina's closer and Admina is farther away, so that's why you see it to the east at midday. It's highest in the sky at dusk, and it sinks to the west in the middle of the night."

"Ummm..."

I used my fists as stand-ins for Cardina and Admina, simulating their positions in relation to the sun.

"Ohhh...I see now. So that's why the moon waxes and wanes over the course of a single night here..."

"Is it different in the real world?"

"Yep. Over there, the moon rotates around Earth—what you'd think of as Cardina—so it waxes and wanes over the course of an entire month."

"Oh, really? I'd like to see that someday," Eolyne said very casually. I didn't know how to respond to it at first.

Everything in the Underworld was contained in the Main Visualizer, and the souls of everyone who lived here were stored in the Lightcube Cluster, both of which were on the *Ocean Turtle*, which was off-limits out at sea near Hachijojima. The ship's nuclear reactor was providing power to the simulation, but if the government decreed the Underworld should be shut down, time would completely stop here, and if it were reinitialized or scrapped altogether, everything and everyone in it would be obliterated without a trace.

No matter what, that was the outcome we absolutely *had* to avoid. But as a measly teenager in high school, I was tragically powerless over that ultimate decision. All I could do was pray that Seijirou Kikuoka and Rinko Koujiro's efforts to ensure the Underworld kept running would pay off...

Actually, no. I was here in the Underworld at Kikuoka's request to investigate the identity of a possible intruder from the Seed Nexus a week ago. If this person was plotting some kind of interference or sabotage, I had to stop them.

Full of fresh determination, I told him, "I'll show it to you. That's a promise."

"Looking forward to it," Eolyne replied, seemingly unbothered by the slight delay in my response. "Altitude of three thousand mels. Rear seat, check fasteners."

I quickly examined my belt once again and said, "All good."

"Main propulsion is active in five, four, three..."

I glanced outside the cockpit again. We'd risen until the craft was at the height of the tallest, wispiest clouds, and I could see not just the End Mountains, but the Dark Territory beyond them, hazy and distant.

"...two, one, launch."

The rumbling that had been modest thus far suddenly turned into a high-pitched scream, like a sports bike at full throttle. I felt my back being pressed into the seat, and the body of the craft vibrated with force. The rumbling didn't feel like wind resistance, but the roaring of the eternal-heat elements inside the engine traveling directly into my body. I'd thought the dragoncraft the girls piloted were extremely fast before, but the power contained within the X'rphan was on a different level entirely.

"Um, i-is it supposed to do this?!" I shouted in a moderate panic.

Eolyne sounded undeniably agitated, too. "I-I'm not sure if this is entirely safe!"

"Maybe we should slow down a bit..."

"But we're still far from top speed!" he informed me. The

engine kicked into the next gear. Clouds ahead of us whipped past in an instant.

I had experience flying in *ALfheim Online*, so I thought being protected by a sturdy, armored dragoncraft would make this experience anything but frightening, but this sense of acceleration was beyond the pale. It took all my self-control not to impulsively hit the brakes with Incarnate power. Instead, I stared dead ahead and emptied my mind.

Suddenly, the sky around us was significantly darker than before. We had somehow risen from level flight into a climb. The Dark Territory surrounding the human realm was encircled by the Wall at the End of the World, which dwarfed the End Mountains separating the two territories. It was said that no living creature, including dragons, could cross that wall, but the dragoncraft were exempt from that definition, and this one raced farther and farther into the heights.

Before long, stars began to twinkle in the sky before us. As the sky went from rich blue to navy, the number of stars increased. The X'rphan continued to soar with absurd speed, but the vibration in the hull was calming down.

"Atmospheric exit complete," Eolyne announced, just as the rumbling calmed down. I lifted my right arm and noticed that I felt almost none of the weight of gravity. Meaning we were in...

"...Outer space?" I muttered. The helmet ahead of me bobbed up and down.

"That's right. Well, I can see why this craft is the stuff of legend...That acceleration earlier was only just over half the output of the main propulsion engine."

"Let's not try the maximum output," I suggested. Up above, in the distant void of space, sat the shining star at the center of the system, Solus.

I'd had to remind myself several times that outer space in the Underworld was not an actual vacuum. For that matter, there wasn't a single oxygen or nitrogen molecule in this entire virtual world. The breeze that brushed my skin and the air going in and out of my lungs was just a sensation the system was simulating for me. So if we were to open the canopy right now, it would be horrendously cold, but we wouldn't suffocate.

Despite that knowledge, however, I couldn't avoid primeval fear. Or perhaps that was a holdover from my experience in *Unital Ring*, suffering the suffocation magic of the witch Mutasina.

I swallowed to dispel that familiar blocked feeling in my throat, and asked Eolyne, "Are we already on the way to Admina now?"

"Yep. Although it's not the most direct route."

"Why not?"

"If we take the default route, we might be spotted by regular ferries and space force craft. Remember, our trip to Admina is a top-secret mission; neither the government nor the Stellar Unification Council knows about it."

"Oh, that's right..."

Eolyne's mission was to find the cause for the sabotage of the Integrity Pilots. My mission was to find out the identity of who had infiltrated the Underworld from the real world and to collect the sealed chest containing the formula for the Deep Freeze art. None of these would be easy objectives to fulfill. When we got there, I had to stay focused on the mission without getting distracted, I told myself.

The pilot seemed to sense my nerves. "You must be tired after all that's happened. It'll take over an hour to reach Admina, so you can recline your seat and relax for a bit."

His consideration and gentle voice were so similar to my late friend that I didn't notice at first that my hands were clenched into fists. I took a deep breath to loosen my nerves, then felt for the reclining bar that would lower the seat back.

"Thanks...In that case, I'll take you up on the offer."

"I'll wake you up if anything happens. Good night, Kirito."

Good night, I replied silently, and closed my eyes.

4

In the sky beyond the window, the distant silver shine grew ever smaller.

Once the light, so small you would never have noticed unless you knew it was there, had passed through the cotton-puff clouds and vanished, Asuna let out the breath she was holding.

Alice was watching the sky right next to her. "So they've gone," she said.

"They've gone," Asuna replied. Alice briefly closed her eyes, saying a silent prayer, then sank deeper into the clear, hot water.

Ten minutes earlier, the silvery dragoncraft left the Morning Star Lookout. After seeing it off, the girls took Airy's suggestion and rushed down to the Great Bath five floors lower. She said it was because they wouldn't be able to see the craft fly away through the trees up there, but they couldn't help but feel that she recognized their secret obsession with baths.

As a matter of fact, the windows in the Great Bath continued all the way to the ceiling and offered a clear view of the blue sky all around them. The vertically rising dragoncraft seemed to be almost translucent somehow, so it was difficult to find, but even the Star King's private vehicle couldn't hide the light of its exhaust. They were thus able to confirm that the dragoncraft made it out to space safely, but as Asuna sank up to her shoulders, she considered that perhaps some random person down in Centoria might have noticed it, too...or perhaps two people, or three.

"Ahhhhh......" The sound escaped her lips. Her body was enveloped in a comfort that relaxed her to the core, even to the inside of her mind. It seemed to her that this had happened before long, long ago.

Actually...it *wasn't* just her imagination. It was on the seventh floor of Aincrad, wasn't it? So nearly four years ago at this point. She and Kirito were at a hotel attached to a massive casino, the hub of a long questline, and they'd taken separate actions at one point—which ended up with her in a gorgeous hotel bath, if not quite as nice as this one. She'd been with Argo the info dealer; an NPC girl who ran the casino; and another NPC, a dark elf knight. She'd looked up to that knight like an older sister and let the woman pour water on her back to wash it off. Then she'd exhibited a mischievous streak unlike most NPCs and skirted her finger down Asuna's spine...

An abrupt pain ran from Asuna's back through her chest, and her breath caught in her lungs. She pushed the memories back down and focused on the sensation of the bath caressing her skin instead.

Thankfully, the pain melted away with time. Those days would never return, and she would never be reunited with that dark elf knight or the other NPCs. But the world of Aincrad, which they'd fought so hard to survive, became the cradle from which the great tree of the Seed Nexus sprang, and the flower that bloomed on the very highest of its branches was the Underworld.

Everything was connected and flowed together. The leaves and branches of that tree had been bundled together into *Unital Ring* to become one. It was almost like the Sefirot, the tree of life in Kabbalah mysticism.

On a whim, she thought about the spelling of Aincrad. Kirito had said that before Akihiko Kayaba's incident was put into motion, it was announced that "Aincrad" was a shortening of "An INCarnating RADius."

But the Sefirot tree started with *Ain*, inspired by *Ayin*, the Hebrew word for nothingness, right? If you cut that off, it left *crad*. She didn't know if that was a syllable or word in Hebrew, but if it were English, the first word that came to mind was *cradle*. Cradle of nothingness.

But in Kabbalah, didn't the infinite come from nothingness? And from infinity comes......

Asuna let that trailing memory end there and sighed. It was pointless trying to decipher the thoughts of Akihiko Kayaba. For the sake of his dream of a truly alternate world, he trapped ten thousand real people, allowed four thousand of them to die, and in the meantime calmly played the role of Heathcliff, leader of the Knights of the Blood. There was no way to understand the thoughts of someone like him.

But when it came to the full-dive system he'd developed and its evolution—Soul Translation—she couldn't help but admit utter wonder.

To this point, she'd experienced countless baths not just in the real world, but in all kinds of VRMMO games, and it felt to her like the baths in the Underworld *surpassed* the real thing. Not only was nothing unnatural about the fluid movement and skin sensation, but the overwhelmingly vivid sense of pleasant relief made it feel as though her soul itself was taking the bath.

But that only made sense; Rath developed the Soul Translator to allow the human soul to access its simulation. However, compared to the previous time she'd been in this particular bath—two months ago in the real world, two hundred years in the Stellar Era calendar—the fidelity of the sensations felt like it had been brought to a whole new level.

If I get too used to this bath, I'm not going to be satisfied by my bath at home anymore, she thought, troubled. It was all just too relaxing.

"Hey! Sti, what are you doing?!" someone shouted, followed by a massive splash.

On the far side of the gargantuan bath, a red-haired girl was swimming this way with a furious dog paddle. The bath was an entire 130 feet long and over 60 feet wide, so it made sense that you might want to swim in it...and then there was another splash.

Just after scolding Stica, Laurannei had chosen to jump into the bath from the hallway in the middle. With perfect form, she soon caught up to her partner and began to break ahead. In response, Stica sped up, and the pilots continued their race past Asuna and Alice in the other direction.

"...I once practiced my swimming in this bath, too. Of course, it was only when the room was empty," Alice muttered under her breath.

Asuna giggled. "When I was a little girl, I swam in the bath at the Kurhaus...which is the name for a huge public bath in the real world. My mother was furious with me."

It was then that Asuna recalled that Alice's parents had died years ago after her childhood in Rulid. She didn't have time to apologize for the comment, however.

"Don't feel bad for me," Alice noted quickly. "I don't have any memories of my early childhood...I can't ask for much more than a chance to be reunited with Selka."

Asuna reached out under the water, trying to touch Alice's hand. When she found it, she squeezed it tight. "Kirito's going to find the sacred art that will undo the petrification. He will."

"Yes, I believe that, too. It's just...," Alice trailed off. As though asking herself as much as anyone else, she continued, "Why did Kirito—the Star King—hide the formula on Admina? If he wanted a safe place, there can't be a safer place than the higher floors of Central Cathedral."

"That's...a good point...," Asuna murmured, gazing across the surface of the water.

A little brown furball swam slowly from right to left, making tiny splashing noises. It was Natsu, Airy's pet. Alice noted dryly, "So...the rat can swim..."

"Long-eared wetrats inhabit the wetlands to the north of the capital," replied Airy, who approached behind Natsu. She folded her arms before her, looking slightly bashful, and explained, "They have webbed toes, so if they swim their hardest, they're even faster than fish."

"Oh, I...didn't know that..."

Natsu reacted to being the center of conversation by dunking under the water. It turned into a dark, barely visible shape that zipped away with astonishing speed. Ahead of it, Stica and Laurannei had turned around at the left end of the bath and were still racing in parallel. Natsu did a turn behind them, sped past them easily, then continued on toward the right end. Just before it reached the goal, it burst out of the water and landed on the marble path, turning to exclaim proudly, *"Kurrrrrr, kyurrr!"*

Asuna, who could not speak rodent language, nevertheless immediately discerned its meaning: "I win!"

That demonstration was enough to defuse the race between Stica and Laurannei, who stared at the victorious Natsu in a daze. After a moment or two, they broke out into applause. Natsu turned around, even prouder than before, puffing out its chest until it fell right onto its back.

"Ha...ha-ha-ha...," Alice chuckled, unable to hold back. Asuna joined her. Even Airy began to laugh, soft and reserved.

As the water around her shook with her laughter, Asuna thought, *I must protect this world. There's no other option. I can't let anyone destroy it before the moment Dr. Koujiro predicted at that press conference a month ago comes true: a world in which real-worlders and Underworlders can interact as equal human beings.*

That's the duty I've been given in exchange for my power as Stacia, Goddess of Creation...

5

At ten AM on Saturday, October 3rd, the first baby was born in the Bashin living quarters on the west side of Ruis na Ríg.

At that time, Silica was in the stables on the north end, feeding the pets. Six days had passed since the start of the *UR* incident, and already the group's pets had grown to quite a selection: Misha, the thornspike cave bear; Kuro, the lapispine dark panther; Aga, the long-billed giant agamid; Namari, the leaden long-tailed eagle; and Silica's partner, Pina.

Fortunately, the four aside from Pina were either omnivorous or carnivorous and would happily eat the harve meat from the Life Harvester, of which they still had mounds and mounds in storage. For the time being, there was no concern over feeding them. She pulled the meat out of her inventory and gave it to Misha, Aga, and Kuro in that order, then the new guy, Namari. She was giving the eagle a luxurious scratch on the soft feathers under its chin when Lisbeth came racing into the stable.

"S-Silica, it's here! It's been born!"

"Wh-what has?!"

"A baby! A baby!"

"Y-yours, Liz?!"

"What?! No, it's not *mine*! Oh, just come with me!"

Lisbeth dragged Silica behind her to the large Bashin tent,

where Silica came face-to-face with a newborn baby in the arms of Yzelma, the Bashin's chieftain.

In Japanese, it was common to describe babies as being "just like a little ball," and no baby Silica had seen before fit that description better than this one, smooth and puffy, rolled up in a blanket. The instant she saw them, she exclaimed, "Awwww!"

The baby slept with utterly sound relief in Yzelma's strong arms, which were as burly as Agil's. Silica looked up at her and asked, "Is this your baby, Yzelma?"

The chieftain smirked and replied, "Did I look like I was *malou* to you? This is the child of Kayatre, wife of Suvor. Kayatre is resting over there after her delivery."

"M-malou? What is that?"

"It means to have a baby in your belly."

"Oh, I see. Malou…malou…"

She kept repeating the brand-new word until at last Yzelma smiled and nodded, and a pop-up appeared, saying, *Bashin skill proficiency has risen to 16.*

In the world of *Unital Ring*, natives like the Bashin, Patter, and Orniths each had their own language. If your proficiency in that language was still zero, the sounds they made were so strange and alien that they couldn't even be expressed in letters, only symbols.

But if you listened patiently, you could sometimes make out sounds that might be repeatable. If you said that sound back to an NPC enough times, and they felt you had pronounced it well enough, your skill proficiency in that language had a chance to rise. Around the time your proficiency was 10, bits of their words would start to sound like Japanese. It was a clever but overly complicated system.

According to Yui the super AI, however, the strange sounds they made at zero proficiency were actually Japanese, just placed under many layers of filters that made them impossible to understand. Yui could analyze and decode the filters on her own, so she was able to understand the Bashin practically from the moment they first met. It was a bit of an unfair advantage, but if not for her, Silica and Lisbeth and Yui quite possibly would not have survived the first night in this world and never reunited with Kirito's group.

In that sense, having the Bashin here in the town and giving birth to new babies was a truly wonderful development, Silica decided. She was savoring this sentiment when Yzelma asked her gently, "Would you like to hold them, Silica?"

"Oh...m-may I?"

"Of course. We Bashin have a saying that a babe held by many heroes will grow up strong and firm. And you are nothing if not a mighty hero."

"Gosh, that's a bit of an exaggeration," she said timidly.

Lisbeth leaned over and smacked her hard on the back. "Don't get all modest on us now! I got a chance to hold the baby earlier, and it was just so...so..."

She seemed to run out of words to describe the sensation, and continued to smack Silica's back instead, so Silica reached out with some reluctance. Yzelma placed the baby in their swaddling cloth right into her hands.

The baby was heavy.

In terms of sheer weight, of course, the materials they used to build the town, like lumber and stone, were much heavier. But the overall weight of the baby, between their sweet scent, softness, and warmth, all felt breathtakingly real in Silica's arms.

Perhaps they didn't like the way she was holding them, because the sleeping baby scrunched up their face a tiny bit and began to murmur. Just when it seemed like they were about to cry, Pina leaned over from Silica's shoulder and rubbed its head against the baby's cheek. The baby seemed to like that texture and stopped fussing, returning to their restful sleep.

"...Does the baby have a name yet?" Silica asked quietly.

Yzelma said, "Yes. Yael."

"Yael...Aww, sweet little Yael...," she cooed, rocking the baby. *I wonder if I'll ever hold my own baby this way*, she thought.

She hoped she would. But it didn't feel like there was anything connecting that future self to her present self. Surely, somewhere and sometime, she would need to choose to leave this comfortable place of hers if she wanted to fall in love, get married, and start a family...

Something's wrong with you, Keiko. You were stuck in bed for two whole years because of that whole crazy thing, and now you're back to playing VR games again. Something's wrong with you.

That was what her old elementary school friend had told her two weeks ago when they ran into each other. She could still hear their words in her head.

The virtual world and the connections she'd fostered in it were more important to Silica than anything. She was certain her friends felt the same way. But maybe it was something akin to a pack of animals that had undergone a long and arduous journey, huddling together in a place of safety and enjoying a much-needed rest together. A mental shelter for those players who'd lived through the harsh reality of *Sword Art Online* and needed a place to heal their wounds.

If so, her companions would probably all leave this place at some point, choosing to take their own paths in life. Asuna and Lisbeth were in their final year at the returnee school and would have college entrance exams in four months. She hadn't asked them what their future plans were, but their time spent logged in was already noticeably lower, and it wasn't certain they would actually come back to hang out together once they had moved on to college.

So in a sense, this *UR* incident might be the last time the whole group of friends would come together as one and fight as a team. Perhaps arriving at the land revealed by the heavenly light, solving all the mysteries, and returning to *ALO* would mark a kind of end point for their collective journey, whether they liked it or not.

It was inevitable. Time was always flowing, and they were becoming closer to adults with each passing day. Everything, no matter how fun, would someday come to an end.

But despite that—no, because *of that…*

Silica silently squeezed the sleeping baby in her arms. If the resolution of the *UR* incident was synonymous with the disappearance of this world, it would mean that everyone who lived here—the Bashin, the Patter, even newborn Yael—would vanish. That was a difficult possibility to accept now that they had forged this trust between them.

Six days ago, under the dazzling aurora in the night sky, Silica heard the voice say, *To the first to reach the land revealed by the heavenly light, all shall be given.*

It was still unclear what "all shall be given" referred to but considering the scale of the abnormality at hand, it couldn't be simple items or stat boosts. But if it *did* turn out to be something like admin status, you might be able to save the NPCs somehow, if not the world itself.

She breathed in one last lungful of the baby's milky scent, then lifted her face. "Yzelma, thank you for letting me hold Yael."

"No, the thanks are all mine," the chieftain replied, plucking the baby out of Silica's arms with a single hand.

As soon as they were out of the tent, Silica and Lisbeth exhaled heavily.

"That baby was soooo cute…"

"Yeah, they sure were…"

"They were making little baby sounds…"

"They sure were…," repeated Lisbeth. Silica glanced over and saw that her face was a melted, whimpering mess. Silica felt the same way, but she couldn't just give in to the temptation to celebrate. Now that both the Bashin and Patter were having new babies, they needed to strengthen Ruis na Ríg's defenses more than ever.

Of course, having defeated their biggest organized foe—Mutasina's army—last night, there shouldn't be any more adversaries seeking to destroy or take over their town anymore, at least among the former *ALO* players. In fact, there were more players coming to Ruis na Ríg since yesterday evening as a waypoint on their adventures; there were currently forty or fifty visitors to the south side of the town, where the shops were set up.

The surprising thing was that the Bashin and Patter had begun conducting trade with the visiting players. The Patter sold only simple meals and rations made from vegetables and legumes harvested from the fields within the living quarters, but the Bashin had armor made from animal pelts and accessories fashioned out of fangs, tusks, and rocks on display, which made for rather exotic-looking storefronts that proved quite popular with the players.

While the overall operator of Ruis na Ríg, Kirito—the settlement had initially been called Kirito Town, after all—indicated that he would not charge the NPCs any fees, the former *Insectsite* and Mutasina army players running lodging houses and shops in the south area were automatically deducted 5 percent of their earnings. If the Bashin business expanded too much, some might complain about an unfair advantage in that regard.

The rules around these dealings should probably be made clear before the town really started expanding in earnest, but the actual leaders of the town—Kirito, Asuna, and Alice—would be absent until later tonight. Hopefully, no trouble would arise while the three of them were gone, Silica thought. She turned to Lisbeth, whose face was still slack with bliss.

"Liz, when do you plan to open your smithy?"

"Huh? Smithee? Oh…right. The smithy."

At last, Lisbeth's mind seemed to return to normal function. She examined the commercial area of the town around her.

"We did a lot yesterday, so I suppose I have enough stock to open up. I'm just a bit worried about the supply of resources, that's all…"

"Resources…meaning ore?"

"Yep. The only nearby iron ore spot is the bear cave to the north, right? Since you tamed Misha, the thornspike cave bears have stopped spawning, so at least it's safe, but the amount of ore you can mine in one go is completely insufficient to supply all of Ruis na Ríg."

"And that iron also needs to go to the buildings and furniture and whatnot..."

"On the other hand, it's typical for iron to be in short supply at the start of an MMO. We struggled with that in Aincrad, too," Lisbeth noted. She stretched and looked up to the sky. Silica followed her gaze.

Time in *Unital Ring* was synced with the real world, so the sky above Ruis na Ríg was a pleasant blue. Beyond the wispy clouds, of course, there was no massive floating castle of steel and rock. New Aincrad had transferred along with Alfheim after the incident started, but with its magical flight suspended, it plummeted to the Battranka Highlands twelve miles to the south and exploded on impact, instantly killing basically every person still inside it.

The majority of the exterior and structure of New Aincrad should have been iron, so it felt like there should be tons of it at the impact site—and not just ore, but refined iron—but according to the players from Mutasina's force, there were incredibly dangerous monsters near that area, making it impossible to reach. Which left one conclusion.

"We've got to find and develop a new gathering point," Silica murmured.

Lisbeth nodded. "That's what it comes down to. Kirito said there was tons of iron ore in the cave behind the waterfall way down the Maruba River, but that's too far to travel, and it'll be trouble for us if that witch finds out about it. I'd prefer a source to the north of our town."

The "witch" Lisbeth spoke of was Mutasina, of course. In the battle two nights ago, the long staff she'd presumably used to cast her horrifying Noose of the Accursed suffocation magic had been destroyed, along with her control over the hundred-strong army she'd amassed. But in the battle, Mutasina, along with her fellow mage Magis, the twin swordswomen Viola and Dia, and the unidentified body double, had all escaped through a smoke screen.

Silica didn't have the chance to either fight or speak with them directly, but she could still remember the horribly realistic sensation of the Noose's choking effect. If Mutasina could use dark magic that powerful, she wasn't likely to give up after a single defeat. She probably couldn't use the Noose again, but they had to assume she was out there somewhere, devising a new plan and sharpening her knives.

"And there should still be thousands of ex-*ALO* players in the Stiss Ruins. If she offers iron equipment as a reward, she could easily put together another force of a hundred or so..."

"If they invade with a group that large right now, I don't think we could totally fight them off," said Lisbeth. They shared a look, then turned to the tent behind them.

Yael was still soundly sleeping inside. In the Patter quarters to the east, the children born in the last few days were all scampering about. It was the humans who had brought these tribes to live here, so it was the humans who were obligated to protect them from outside enemies.

"...Liz, do you want to go exploring a bit to the north?"

"I was just going to suggest the same thing."

They shared another look, then grinned.

In *Unital Ring*, where a single death was the end of the game, it was forbidden to do anything risky and reckless, but that didn't mean they could stay hide in town forever. Silica and Lisbeth were both level-16, which was on the higher end among the group, although Kirito was already over level-20, after all the boss monsters he'd been fighting. They needed to close that gap by a level or two while he was away.

Others would be logging in soon, too. If they could get together a party of four, plus Pina and Misha, that should be plenty enough power for exploring the forest.

Silica and Lisbeth started picking up the pace, and before long they were outright sprinting for the log cabin.

The thing was, VRMMOs were just plain fun. The thrill of heading into unknown territory with your friends was a feeling that nothing else could replace.

If it was meant to end someday, then all the more reason to enjoy it to the fullest now.

Atop Silica's head, seemingly absorbing her newfound determination, Pina spread its wings and cried, *"Kweei!"*

6

After chopping up all the veggies left in the fridge, frying them a bit, and simmering them with canned tomatoes for a simple minestrone, then eating the soup with leftover bâtard bread for a late breakfast, Shino Asada was ready to plan her day.

Kirito, Asuna, and Alice would be investigating in the Underworld from morning until evening, so the heavy work in *Unital Ring* wouldn't start until seven o'clock. She'd finished virtually all of Friday's homework last night, except for the workbook material in Classical Literature B. In *ALO* she could bring her homework into the game and have a study session with her friends, asking for help when needed and having fun all the while, but *Unital Ring* had no feature to import outside file contents.

She always prioritized her schoolwork, and besides, she couldn't truly enjoy a game with 100 percent of her concentration if the thought of some unfinished homework was in the back of her mind. So she should focus on her workbook in the morning and save her dive until the afternoon. Despite this, however, she couldn't help but feel curious about the current state of Ruis na Ríg.

If her game performance was going to suffer because of thinking about homework, and she couldn't focus on her homework because she was wondering about the game, then the latter would probably represent a worse betrayal of her studies, she decided. So maybe it would be best to zip through Ruis na Ríg, confirm that the town was functioning properly, and then focus on her homework with all qualms cleared up.

I feel like I'm starting to think the way Kirito does, she realized. But it didn't stop her from putting on the AmuSphere and lying down in bed.

"Link Start," she announced, feeling a bit guilty. *It's just one loop of the town!* she told herself, passing through the tunnel of light and emerging in the living room of the log cabin as Sinon the sniper.

"Back row acquired!" someone shouted, tugging on her collar from behind.

"*Unnyaa?!*" she squealed. "Wh-what was that?!"

She spun around and saw Silica and Klein standing side by side. The one who'd grabbed her turned out to be Lisbeth.

"...What's going on here?" Sinon asked, blinking suspiciously.

Silica gave her an innocent smile. "Good morning, Sinon! We're about to go exploring in the forest to the north. Would you like to join us?"

"I—I was only coming in to do a quick patrol of the town," Sinon explained before realizing that this was the sort of question in which only the answer yes would result in her collar being released. "Uhhh...er, all right. As long as it doesn't take too long."

"Nooo, not long at all!" Klein beamed. "We're just doin' a liiiittle bit of mapping!"

"Yep! And then searching for a teeeeensy bit of iron ore while we're there!" Lisbeth added.

Why do I find that hard to believe? Sinon thought, even as she said, "Okay, fine."

The party of four topped off their consumable items, stopped by the stable to add Misha, the thornspike cave bear, to their number, then left the town through the Two O'Clock Gate to the northeast.

Yui wasn't with them because she was spending the majority of her processing resources on monitoring the network while Kirito and Asuna were investigating the Underworld. That meant not a single member of Team Kirito was left behind in Ruis na Ríg, although there were several members of the *Insectsite* group, and besides, if they started seriously pushing forward, they wouldn't have the luxury of leaving people in town anyway. Ruis na Ríg was functioning well as a waypoint now, and they'd just have to pray that no violent ruffians came by and tried to destroy the town.

Thirty yards north of the gate, the little path they'd built for transporting lumber ended, leaving nothing but untouched natural forest before them. It was a grand sight, as the name Great Zelletelio Forest suggested, but unlike real forests, the undergrowth wouldn't block your progress. The ground was covered in soft grasses and dotted in warm, dappled light that filtered through the branches, like a scene from an Ivan Shishkin painting.

"Mmm, gotta love a good forest!" opined Klein, who stretched luxuriously. From the rear line behind him, Misha, the thorn-spike cave bear, agreed, growling, *"Gruhhh..."*

It felt nice, that was true, but this wasn't a picnic trip. "You're here to help us explore, right, Klein?" said Sinon.

"And you need to be looking for iron ore sources, too," snapped Lisbeth.

The katana-wielder gave them a massive thumbs-up. "I'm on it! The only things that don't get picked up on my sensor are ghosts and chameleons."

"You seem awfully convinced that we won't see any ghosts in the middle of the day," Sinon noted dryly. Klein protested, claiming that surely there wouldn't be any daytime ghosts, but all the same, his eyes swiveled around the surroundings with a higher frequency after that.

At the very least, they knew from Kirito and Alice that the world of *Unital Ring* did contain astral-type undead monsters.

Four days ago, they'd gone to meet up with Argo at the Stiss Ruins, where they unintentionally met the requirements to encounter a quest monster called a vengeful wraith, a fight that nearly proved fatal.

The condition to run across the wraith was to have a silver item manifested on your person. The silver coin Sinon had given to Alice did the trick, apparently. She'd given the silver coin to her to try to buy any musket bullets and gunpowder they might be selling at the ruins. Unfortunately, there were no such items available.

Bullets could be fashioned out of iron, so there wasn't any concern of running out of ammo—the problem was gunpowder. According to the Ornith siblings who gave Sinon her musket, the explosive was made by mixing charcoal powder with the secretions of an insect called a bursting beetle.

Bursting beetles were found at the foot of cacti growing on the west end of the Giyoru Savanna, but that was over eighteen miles from Ruis na Ríg, and there was a massive natural rock formation like the Great Wall of China in between that further complicated travel.

She had about sixty uses of gunpowder left. Once that was gone, she'd have to use the Bellatrix SL2 optical gun dropped by a former *Gun Gale Online* player who'd died shortly after coming into this game. But of course, she couldn't recharge its energy stock, so that would eventually run out, too. She needed to find a means to produce gunpowder sooner rather than later…

These thoughts occupied her mind on their trek through the beautiful forest environment, and before long, there was a low vibration audible ahead of them.

Misha uttered a short, quiet alert. Up front, Klein and Lisbeth came to a stop.

Vmmmmm…It sounded like the hum of a large mechanical monster from *GGO*, except the pitch was rising and falling ever so slightly. Nothing could be seen yet because of the curtains of vines hanging from the branches of the ancient trees around them.

Klein held a finger to his lips for silence, then pointed to a spot where the curtain of greenery was thinnest. The others followed him and snuck forward in silence.

After parting the vines, they found that the shrubbery ahead formed a kind of arched tunnel. The vibration was coming from somewhere down the tunnel. It was just wide enough for Misha to pass through, but the bear wasn't going to be able to nimbly back up, which would cause trouble if any monsters came charging down the tunnel at them.

With some more hand signs, they elected Sinon and Klein to perform recon. They headed into the tunnel, examining the dense shrubbery around them. The thick, intertwined branches were bristling with thorns. It was most likely an indestructible piece of terrain that would cause damage on contact. The thorny brush ran east to west for quite a long way and was clearly dividing the forest into two sections.

Fortunately, the tunnel itself was only about thirty feet long. The other exit was also covered by vines, and it was beyond there that the undulating vibration was coming from.

Klein and Sinon lined up and carefully pulled aside the curtain with a fingertip.

"Eugh!" he promptly exclaimed. Sinon would have scolded him because he had been the one who shushed them all first, if not for the fact that she understood his feeling.

The tunnel ended in a domed space about fifty yards across. In the middle was the largest and oldest tree they'd seen yet in *Unital Ring*, and the ground was dotted with massive, rafflesia-like flowers with petals in toxic colors. But neither of those things were what elicited Klein's disgusted reaction.

The tree's knotted trunk and gnarled branches were swallowed up by a dark-brown mass. It was made up of elliptical shapes covered with a scale-shaped, striped pattern—just like a wasp's nest.

Except these shapes were each easily over fifteen feet across, five or six of them fused together, like some kind of wasp apartment building.

Naturally, the residents of this apartment were gigantic wasps.

From holes all over the structure emerged twenty-inch-long wasps, busily milling about. Their bodies were a dark metallic green, with light-brown wings. Each one sported a long, slightly curved stinger from its bottom.

Upon leaving the nest, the wasps buzzed loudly about the dome before landing on one of the rafflesia flowers and sticking their heads into the center. After a few moments, each wasp would fly back to the nest. Sinon and Klein couldn't begin to imagine how many there were in total.

"This could be big trouble for us if we're not careful," Klein whispered. *That's true for most monsters*, Sinon thought but nodded to show her agreement. Let happy wasps lie. They should retreat with haste—but the problem was that, based on the landscape around them, the wasp nest dome was most likely the only...

"Hey, you two."

Sinon was taken by such surprise that she raised her musket out of sheer reflex. Eyes darting left and right, she saw, lurking in a kind of natural evacuation zone surrounded by rocks and shrubs near the wall to the right, a man.

He was this close, and I didn't notice him. Very good Hiding skill, Sinon noted with frustration. In *Unital Ring*, staring at a player did not produce an automatic cursor, but she did recognize his face. He was a former *ALO* player who was captured by the *Insectsite* group while scouting on Mutasina's behalf. And his name was...

"Oh, is that you, Friscoll?" Klein hissed. The man nodded and waved them closer.

If Friscoll had been observing the wasp dome, it would be well worth hearing what he had to say, but the others were still waiting at the mouth of the tunnel. Their impatience meter was probably about to hit its limit. If they didn't go back soon, the others would come marching down the tunnel with Misha.

Sinon beckoned to him and whispered, "You come with us."

Friscoll made a face but acquiesced. He watched the nest carefully, then crawled out of the evacuation zone, slithering almost silently along the wall to the tunnel.

At last he stood up, and it became clear that he was wearing a very strange outfit, indeed. It was a hooded robe that covered his entire body, but the faded green cloth was adorned with many fluffy linen strips, almost like a ghillie suit for snipers. In fact, it was probably designed for that exact purpose.

"What? Oh, this?" Friscoll grinned, noticing the way Sinon was staring at him. "Pretty nice, huh? The rats—er, the Patter back at Ruis na Ríg sell them. They said it takes four days to make a single suit."

"Oooh…"

Impressed, Sinon started to make a note to buy a suit the next time they finished one, then reminded herself that now was not the time. She and Klein followed Friscoll back down the tunnel; Sinon apologized to Silica and Lisbeth for leaving them waiting and explained what they'd found. Both girls loudly grimaced.

"Wasps, huh?"

"They *are* familiar enemies, though…"

As Silica said, wasp- and bee-type monsters were common in both *ALO* and *GGO*, and presumably in *SAO* as well. But that didn't mean they were easy pickings. They had three major danger attributes—flight, poison, and groups—so most games tended to peg them as dangerous foes in the early-to-mid game sections.

On that note, Klein rubbed at his stubble and commented, "They're bad news, guys. That nest was the size of a freakin' house. Best move is probably to go around them."

"I knew you'd say that, old man," said Friscoll, who was mysteriously cocky, with a smirk. Klein snapped, "You're basically the same age as me!" but the man was unbothered by it.

"You guys know how the *UR* world is structured by now, right?" he asked.

"Yes…it's a circular map with a radius of over four hundred miles, with all the VRMMO players arranged along the outside and the goal in the very center," she said, quoting Argo.

Friscoll smirked again. "You're mostly right but a little out of date."

He scooped up a dead branch off the ground, then used it to draw a circle in some exposed dirt. Then he added another circle on the inside, then another.

"If you combine what all the Seed game players are saying, you'll find out it's not just a simple flat circle, but a tiered structure with the goal at the middle."

"Tiered…like a wedding cake, you mean?" Silica asked.

"That's right. Like concentric circles." Friscoll said, speaking faster with excitement. "If the radius is over four hundred miles, then for every sixty miles or so heading inland from the shoreline at the very outer edge, it gets another step taller. And after the next length, it gets taller again. There's a cliff just north of the Stiss Ruins, and the difference is, like, six or seven times the height of the ruins. It was easily over six hundred feet. Of course, at scale on the map, it'll look like the width of a piece of paper, but in person, you'd have to be suicidal to attempt free-climbing it."

"Then how do you get up there?" Lisbeth asked. Once again, Friscoll grinned.

"I'd prefer to charge you for anything else…but given that I owe you a debt for freeing me from Muta-Muta's bastard magic, I'll tell you for free."

Muta-Muta was Mutasina presumably. If she found out he was calling her that, she'd probably come straight here to murder him, but that was his problem to deal with, so Sinon ignored the comment and prompted, "And?"

"Listen, this is ultra-rare intel, so don't go blabbing this to any old person you meet. There are actually places designed for you to get up to the next step. Usually, it's a dungeon that goes inside the cliff face, but some of them are stairs carved into the rock or rickety old ladders that could fall apart at any moment."

Friscoll wore an expression that said this was incredibly sensitive information he was passing on, but it all sounded quite commonsense. It wouldn't be much of a game if you were faced with unscalable cliffs and had no route to safely get up.

He could clearly sense they were thinking this from their facial expressions, so he hastily added, "But they also say there's always some super-dangerous barrier arranged along each route to get up the next cliff step. Like puzzles that cause you to die if you fall off or field bosses powerful enough to wipe out a whole thirty-man raid party."

"And…that wasp nest is our field boss in this case?" Sinon asked.

Friscoll pursed his lips. "Yep, no doubt about it. I've traveled east and west from the tunnel mouth for a while, and these thorny bushes just continue forever. No blades or fire can harm the stuff. I'm thinkin' that waspy area is supposed to be the first checkpoint for everyone who started at the ruins."

"Ah, I see…"

This information aligned with Sinon's observations. Unless they figured out some way to get past the wasp nest dome, they would never reach the land revealed by the heavenly light…

On the other hand, there was another solution, one that was definitely not the "proper" answer.

"But if what you said is true, then if we keep going either east or west for long enough, we should find the barrier and cliff for the players from a different game. If they've already broken through that barrier, couldn't we just trace their route up to the next step?"

"Uh…well, sure," Friscoll said, crossing his arms. It made all the frills on his ghillie suit wiggle. "From what I hear, some folks have already broken through the first barrier."

"Are you serious?!" yelped Klein, stepping closer. "Which game was it?"

"Tsk. All right, but this is the limit of what I can tell ya. I've only heard it secondhand, haven't confirmed it myself, but from what I hear, as of this morning, two groups have broken through the first barrier. The first one is called *Apocalyptic Date*, a game where all the players are anthro."

"Oh! I've heard of *AD*!" Silica reacted instantly. Her triangular ears twitched with excitement. "All the avatars are so cute and fluffy! Though I've heard there are reptiles and amphibians, too...I was thinking of converting over to try it out sometime."

"Now, listen up, little miss. They might look cute, but they're fierce fighters. The reason they've been making quick progress is because their fur and claws are so tough, they've only needed to do the minimum of equipment production," Friscoll pointed out, eliciting a puffy-cheeked pout from Silica.

"As long as you look cute, the rest doesn't matter! Anyway, what's the other game?"

"Oh, this one's famous, so you'd probably recognize it," Friscoll prefaced. In hushed tones for dramatic effect, he revealed, "It's *Asuka Empire*."

"......"

The group shared a look. Even Sinon, who didn't know much about any VRMMOs except *GGO* and *ALO*, knew what sort of a game that one was. It featured a beautiful world design with a traditional Japanese motif and had character classes like samurai, ninja, monk, and miko. It was so popular among gamers that its active playerbase was nearly as large as *ALO*'s.

"But...unlike *AD*, *Asuka* would have to make their own equipment. How did they get so far ahead?"

"If you want the simple answer, it's because they didn't get bogged down in BS," Friscoll told Klein, arms folded. He shrugged. "Thanks to Muta-Muta, us *ALO* players had a huge infighting problem, and that was true of most of the game groupings. On our left, *GGO* was getting into gunfights over ammo, and on our right, *Insectsite* was fighting between Sixes and Eighmores, right? Basically, no game population can really focus on conquering the game until the fight over hegemony is settled. For whatever reason, the *Asuka Empire* folks settled on a cooperative stance right at the start and set up a huge production center near their starting point."

"……"

The group fell silent again. In the past six days, the former *ALO* players had, as Friscoll put it, a "huge infighting problem." But that was clearly because the witch Mutasina and her companions immediately began plotting against the others, cast a massive Noose of the Accursed spell to enslave an army of a hundred players, and attempted to seize control over any rivals.

Mutasina's ambitions were foiled for now, but her influence still heavily colored the population. More than a few players had given up on playing again, intimidated by the possibility of being afflicted by the Noose.

Perhaps this slowdown will prove fatal for us, Sinon thought, biting her lip.

"Hey, don't get down, Sino-Sino," said Friscoll, the very person who had just given her all this depressing information, smacking her on the shoulder. "Yeah, *Asuka* and *AD* have a big lead, but we've got a huge advantage on our side, too."

"…What advantage is that?"

"Ruis na Ríg, of course! Not a single other game has such a large and advanced base built as far ahead as we do: nearly twenty miles from the starting point. If we can break through that waspy-wasp area today, our supply train logistical advantage should help us make up a ton of ground on those other two groups."

"……Well, you may be right about that," Sinon agreed, nodding slowly. With its helpful magic spells, *ALO* made it surprisingly easy to just grind through long questlines, but in *GGO*, you needed ammo, energy packs, and med kits, so when tackling a major quest far from town, you had to start by setting up a campsite out in the wilderness.

Magic skills existed in *Unital Ring*, but for the moment, they couldn't generate water and food. In order to travel to the center of the world, you'd need to travel between your progress point and a production hub several times. That made the presence of a massive forward base like Ruis na Ríg extremely beneficial.

The town had grown to its current size only because Kirito and Asuna and Alice had fought so hard to protect the log cabin that had fallen out of New Aincrad. The three of them wouldn't be back until tonight, so the rest of the group was obligated to carry their own weight by making further progress until then.

"...All right. Let's break through that wasp dome," Sinon announced. Klein, Lisbeth, Silica, and Friscoll all grinned at her words. She glared swiftly at the last of them, who was acting like he was a long-term member of the team already, and added, "Also, if you call me Sino-Sino one more time, I'm going to find out if that ghillie suit is as flammable as it looks."

7

C'mon, Kirito. Wake up.

The sound of someone whispering near my ear caused my eyes to slide open.

There was immediately a full curtain of stars before my eyes. *Did I fall asleep outside?* I wondered groggily, until I noticed the gentle vibration running through my body.

I wasn't indoors *or* outdoors. I was inside the cockpit of the dragoncraft X'rphan Mk. 13.

Ahead of me was Commander Eolyne's helmet, visible in the pilot seat. He was totally still, not because he was sleeping, but out of concentration. I didn't want to bother him, so I leaned my head back against the headrest.

I closed my eyes and tried to recall the dream I was having before I woke up, but my memory was as delicate as a snowflake in the hot sun and melted clean away. I exhaled in frustration, and right on cue, a gentle voice said, "Did you wake up, Kirito?"

"Y-yeah. How could you tell?" I asked, bolting upright.

"I wouldn't make a very good commander if I didn't notice small details like that," he said. I couldn't tell if he was serious or joking. Eolyne pointed to the left of the craft's nose. "Look, we're nearly there."

I raised the seat back to its upright position and looked where he was pointing through the canopy. Immediately, I grunted, "Whoa…"

Down below the craft on the left was a massive spherical body. It was difficult to grasp size and distance in space, but there was no doubt this was Admina, our destination.

It glowed a soft yellow where the sunlight hit it, and the opposite side was utterly dark, which told me this was indeed the same body, Lunaria, that I had seen from the human realm two hundred years ago. I had a vague memory of talking to someone about the possibility of there being people living in cities on the moon, but I couldn't remember who it was.

"…How many people live on that planet…?" I asked softly.

Eolyne whispered back, "About five thousand, between five races."

"Whoa…that's it? Just five thousand on an entire planet…?"

"The human realm and dark realm have more than enough space for everyone, and there's also the Outer Continent beyond the Wall at the End of the World. It's almost entirely undeveloped. With the greenification of the Dark Territory proceeding well, very few people would actually desire to move to Admina."

"But if the settlers there have children…," I protested.

Enigmatically, Eolyne replied, "Having children won't change the overall population."

"Huh…?"

"The number of those who leave the world and enter the world is always the same…Isn't that the way it works in the real world, too?"

His meaning eluded me at first, and I spent several long moments blinking in confusion before I finally understood.

The Underworld had a hard population limit.

The souls of the people here, their fluctlights, were all stored within the Lightcube Cluster on the *Ocean Turtle*. The total number of cubes in the cluster was around two hundred thousand, as I recalled, so there couldn't be more fluctlights than that.

Two hundred years ago, the population of the human realm

was eighty thousand, so if the Dark Territory's was around the same, it would leave only forty thousand unused cubes. With no more war plaguing the world, that leftover slack would be filled up in no time—and that was indeed what had happened, it seemed. The population of the Underworld had reached two hundred thousand, its physical limit, so unless someone died so their cube could be reinitialized, there would be no new souls to load in. That was what Eolyne meant by "the number of those who leave the world and enter the world is always the same."

"...No, there's no limitation of that sort in the real world," I replied, drawing a suspicious look from the pilot commander.

"Huh...? Then your population will simply grow and grow without end?"

"Yes, that's right," I confirmed. He would just have to take my word on this one. "In the real world, the total population is over eight billion."

"Eight......"

Even coolheaded Eolyne was frozen for a good three seconds after that one. He turned as far to the left as he could, until his shocked face was visible over the side of the pilot's chair, which sat slightly lower than mine.

"D-did you say eight billion? As in, ten thousand times eight hundred thousand?"

"Ummm, hang on," I said, trying to count up the zeroes in my head. "Yeah. Ten thousand times eight hundred thousand."

"......Goodness gracious," he murmured, shaking his head and turning forward again. "It is written that during the Otherworld War, an army of tens of thousands of real-worlders came here, so I had a feeling you must have a higher population...but in the billions? Which means that if..."

He caught himself there and muttered, "Er, never mind."

I was on the denser side, but even I could guess at what Eolyne was about to say: If a new Otherworld War broke out, and the Underworld and real world had a conflict far greater than the one from two centuries ago, it would be two hundred thousand versus eight billion.

Lieutenant Colonel Kikuoka, Dr. Koujiro, Alice, Asuna, and I and all of our friends were working hard not to let that happen, but I couldn't be irresponsible enough to guarantee that we could prevent a war. So I inhaled, let it out slowly, then changed the topic: "Is a day on Admina the same length as on Cardina?"

"Yes, it is. But the position of Ori, the capital of Admina, is the polar opposite of Centoria's, so it's the middle of the night there."

"Ori..."

I pondered what the source of the name might be but had no idea. If Yui were here, she'd be able to list a whole load of potential sources from different languages, but she was busy monitoring the network while Asuna, Alice, and I were in this dive. Plus, she couldn't log in to the Underworld anyway.

Upon a closer examination of the night side of Admina, I could see flickers of what looked like man-made light. But the dragoncraft was not heading straight for them; it seemed to be pointed at a spot far to the east of there.

"Ummm...I'm guessing we can't just go and land right on the pad in town?" I asked.

Naturally, Eolyne replied, "Of course not. Even with our deceptive measures, there's no hiding the light of the craft's exhaust."

"So if we land a long distance away, how are we getting to the city?"

"What are those big, long legs for, Kirito?"

Are you serious? Also, they're not that long.

He chuckled, seemingly reading my mind, and pushed the control stick forward.

The silvery dragoncraft began a smooth descent toward the boundary line between day and night.

The reason for Admina's yellow color turned out to be a surprising one.

I had assumed it was the color of the atmosphere, but on the ground, the sky was the same clear blue as on Cardina. It was the majority of the surface that was colored pale yellow—it was covered in yellow flowers, to be precise.

As the craft descended to three thousand feet, I stared at the flower fields stretching all the way to the horizon in absolute wonder.

"Did...did people plant these flowers?"

"No, it was already this way the first time the Star King landed here," Eolyne explained, as though he'd been expecting this question. "It's hard to tell from this height, but there is actually a mixture of several kinds of yellow flowers growing there. The particular species change depending on the season, so Admina appears yellow all year round."

"Huh..."

It was tempting to say that if someone at Rath had designed Admina's terrain, they were slacking off, but I had a feeling that was not the case. Most likely, as soon as someone from the Underworld—the Star King, as the story went—approached Admina, the heavenly body previously called Lunaria, the Cardinal System generated its own detailed map for the planet. If so, then only Cardinal, the sage from the library, could possibly say why it chose this particular design—but she no longer existed. The only remaining traces of her and Administrator, her offshoot, were the names of the two planets.

I took my eyes off the endless flowers to look at the sky ahead of us. The spectrum spanned from red to navy blue, not as a sunset but as a sunrise. Our backs were to the rising sun, and we were flying toward the night. There was no artificial light visible ahead of us yet.

"...Hey, if we're sneaking up on the capital, wouldn't it be better to do it from the night side, rather than the day side?" I asked.

"Well, yes, but in order to do so, we'd have to spin all the way around the planet," Eolyne explained, tracing the path with his finger, "which would take twice as long. But we've come on a course that ensures the curvature of the planet blocks the city from seeing us, so the chances of being detected are almost infinitesimally small...I think."

True, at the spot where the dragoncraft entered the atmosphere, there was absolutely no way to see the light of the city. And there was no radar or satellites in this world. The only means of long-distance observation were massive telescopes, which meant detecting dragoncraft that were just tiny dots in the vast sky would be incredibly difficult.

The X'rphan Mk. 13 glided over the yellow fields of flowers, sounding so smooth, you'd never guess it had just been dusted off from a decades-long slumber. Even the occasional tree we passed had all-yellow leaves. I wished I could show this to Asuna and Alice, but the dragoncraft seated only two. If we completed our mission on Admina and managed to wake Selka, Ronie, and Tiese, we should eventually have the chance to visit this planet as a group.

As the craft traveled onward, the red in the sky moved behind us, and the dark of night grew larger. That meant we were flying faster than Admina's rotational speed. Yet there was almost no sensation of air resistance. Either because it was just a virtual world or because of some special property of the dragoncraft.

I did seem to recall that when I tried flying at maximum speed with Incarnation during the Otherworld War, I'd had to make a wind-element barrier to keep from being absolutely buffeted. So even without the existence of air molecules, the system still simulated the concept of wind resistance. That meant this dragoncraft had to have some kind of mechanism similar to a wind-element barrier. In fact, when we had plunged into the atmosphere from space, there weren't any of those usual signs of atmospheric entry you saw in movies and anime, like the ship glowing red or shaking itself to pieces.

"Hey, Eolyne...," I said, about to ask the illustrious pilot commander how the craft was canceling out the wind resistance, when an urgent alarm filled the cockpit without warning, and red lights turned on here and there on the instrument board.

"Wh-what's that?!" I yelped in a panic.

His response was tense but controlled. "An Incarnation reading. Did you do something, Kirito?"

"N-no, I didn't do anything!"

"Then it's an attack. I'll look above us. You keep an eye on what's below."

"G-got it!"

I had so many questions—*Who's attacking? Why? How?*—but the situation was too urgent to bother him with them. I just kept my eyes peeled, alternating between left and right below the craft.

On the left side ahead, right around the boundary between night and evening, I saw a number of red lights approaching our position.

"I've got lights at ten o'clock!" I shouted, then worried he might not understand clock positions.

Fortunately, Eolyne replied, "Yes, I have visual! Those are… Incarnate-guided missiles. It's gonna get bumpy!"

A high-pitched whine arose around us. The X'rphan shuddered like a living thing, then shot upward and to the right, as though it had been struck. I was pressed so hard into the seat that I could feel my body creaking. I'd thought our acceleration when leaving Cardina was the craft's maximum, but the Star King's personal vehicle was capable of more. We moved so fast that I could barely breathe, but I was still able to turn my head and look through the clear canopy behind us.

The red lights were still clearly visible. In fact, they seemed to be creeping closer.

"We're not pulling away, Eolyne!"

"I didn't think so! Let me know if they get within five hundred mels!"

How do I tell? I thought. But despite the blank canvas of the sky, with no other indicators of depth, I found that I could accurately perceive the distance between us and the lights. Seven hundred mels…six hundred…

"Five hundred!" I shouted, and the engine roared once again.

The craft did a backflip at an extreme angle, practically launching itself off of thin air. I was momentarily terrified that the delicate X'rphan might break apart, but the force pressing me against the seat made it clear that the frame beneath us was indomitably firm.

Gritting my teeth against the pressure, I stared at the gloom overhead. I could catch a red gleam out of the corner of my eye. There were at least twelve or thirteen of these Incarnate-guided missiles. About a third of them seemed to have lost sight of us and went veering off in other directions, but the other two-thirds made the turn like living things and continued pursuit.

"Is…is someone controlling them?!" I cried.

Even in this dire situation, Eolyne made sure to answer my question. "No, they're Incarnate weapons that automatically track their target! Somewhere there's a mechamobile or dragoncraft that fired…them!"

He rolled the craft to the right and banked into another sharp turn. Another few guided missiles lost their bead on us and fell away, but five or six still stayed on us. They were less than three hundred mels away now. At this distance, I could see that they were tubelike objects made of gray metal—exactly like regular missiles. The red light was because of a lenslike part on the tip of each projectile.

They were each over three feet long, which seemed very small in comparison to real-life air-to-air missiles. But if an object that size exploded close enough, even the X'rphan was bound to take some damage. I kept an eye on our rear and warned Eolyne, "If it looks like it's going to hit us, I'm using Incarnation!"

"I suppose you won't have a choice. Just keep the effect to a minimum!"

It seemed, based on the reaction, that our assailants already knew we were here, but it wasn't clear if they knew we were the Integrity Pilot commander and the former Star King or just thought we were unidentified trespassers. If the latter, using my

Incarnation at full power would essentially be announcing my identity for all to see.

The X'rphan did a third loop, dropping the number of missiles in pursuit down to three. But they were now less than two hundred mels away. If we kept trying to loop and lost enough speed, they would make up all that distance, and we'd be unable to get away.

There were two ways I could stop them with Incarnation: I could generate a ton of heat elements through the canopy and attack with them, or I could set up a simple defensive wall in the same way. It would feel good to shoot them out of the sky, but if it caused a huge explosion, the blast range might reach us.

Best to just rely on a barrier, I decided, and told Eolyne, "I'm defending us!" Then I generated an Incarnate wall that surrounded the craft, only a tenth as strong as when I'd blocked the Abyssal Horror's light beam.

Half a second later, the three guided missiles made contact with the wall in quick succession.

There was an explosion. Then another.

A yellow flash filled the evening sky. The blast spread out along a ball-shaped surface, the contour of the Incarnate wall I'd made. There was some level of feedback on me from the shock wave of the explosion, but the force was only as much as five or six heat elements bursting at once—a far cry from the spacebeast's attacks.

Three guided missiles made contact with the wall, but there were only two explosions. The third one was either destroyed before it could detonate or got tossed far, far away, I guessed. Just in case, I kept the wall deployed as I informed Eolyne, "All guided projectiles remo—"

Before I could finish, something with an alien texture, chilly or perhaps slimy, licked my conscious mind.

Something was trying to wriggle through the Incarnate wall. It felt like something eroding the firm, hard wall I created in my

imagination, gouging a tiny hole and infiltrating through it. Like some kind of parasite sheathed in a viscous lubricant.

I twisted around and stared over my right shoulder. In a corner of the sky, now that the blast had almost entirely faded, writhed a very bizarre object. A long, black, tubelike object about three feet long and two inches wide. It was not a weapon made of metal, but a living thing, like a snake or a worm, but at the same time, not exactly either.

Its eyeless, mouthless tip was glowing red from the inside. The other guided missiles were definitely just made of gray metal, so this happened to be the one living-type weapon out of the bunch, as far as I could tell.

The black earthworm had already wriggled about half its body through the Incarnate wall. I reached out with my left hand and tried to close the hole, but no matter how much pressure I added, the secretion coating the earthworm's body seemed to just melt the Incarnation. I had no idea it was possible to do such a thing, but Incarnation was basically just a manipulation of matter through the power of imagination. Eolyne mentioned Incarnation-Hiding Incarnation earlier; if Incarnation-Eroding Incarnation also existed, then I could make my wall as strong as I could, and it would have no effect on that bioweapon.

Eolyne seemed to have noticed the writhing black worm in empty space, too. He couldn't conceal the disgust in his voice. "Wh-what *is* that thing?"

"Don't ask me. Also…it's going to get inside our defensive wall soon!"

"Got it. Hold out just a bit longer," he said, and pressed his left hand against the canopy shield.

Ten glowing blue frost elements appeared on the outside of the thick glass. It was an ultra-high-level technique, not only eschewing the spoken command but also ignoring the basic rule of sacred arts that one must generate a single element with each finger.

He waved his hand, and the frost elements shot toward the

black earthworm, leaving behind blue trails. The instant they made contact, it created huge masses of ice.

In just seconds, the front half of the earthworm that had infiltrated the defensive wall was trapped inside a floating iceberg. Eolyne's Incarnation was controlling the elements, but the ice itself was solid, so a substance that invaded Incarnation shouldn't be able to melt it. Sure enough, while the back half of the worm was still struggling and writhing, the front half was completely still. The warnings in the cockpit continued blaring; they probably wouldn't turn off as long as the worm was alive.

"Okay...I'm going to land the X'rphan now. Keep that defensive wall up," Eolyne instructed.

I nodded nervously. "G-got it."

Having the black earthworm violating my Incarnation felt horrible, but I'd have to put up with it for now. Just in case, I imagined the defensive wall around the earthworm being even stronger.

But right on cue, just as I did that, I felt another slithering, slippery feeling from directly below.

By the time I realized what was happening, a long, soft body had penetrated the Incarnate wall.

"Eolyne! It came from below—!" I shouted, but before I could finish my thought, a massive explosion drowned me out.

8

Asuna felt something prickle the back of her neck and stopped short.

She turned and saw the great stairs, lined with thick red carpet, but nothing out of the ordinary. There was a feeling of disquiet in her chest when she faced forward again and saw that Alice had also stopped and was looking strangely at her.

"...Asuna, did something just...?"

"You felt it, too...?" she whispered back.

They peered around again, but the marble walls that made up Central Cathedral completely separated the inside and outside of the structure, leaving only a centuries-old silence to fill the dim stairway.

"Asuna, Alice, what's the matter?" asked a voice from farther up the stairs. Stica and Laurannei were waiting at the next landing, looking curiously down at them. Airy stood beyond them, holding Natsu, but none of them seemed to have felt anything amiss.

"Sorry, it's nothing!" Asuna replied, and the two hurried up the steps.

After seeing off Kirito and Eolyne in their dragoncraft, the girls had gone to the Great Bath on the ninetieth floor to wash off the sweat of the day, then put on thin bathrobes in the changing room lounge nearby, drank cold beverages, and ate fruit as they talked.

When the one-thirty bells rang, they decided to change back into their clothes and left the bath. Their next destination was the kitchen on the ninety-fourth floor, to prepare a big feast for when Kirito and Eolyne returned. The current topic of discussion was what to make.

The men wouldn't come back until at least four o'clock, so there was plenty of time to work with. According to Airy, Asuna had spent lots of time in this kitchen as the Star Queen, developing new dishes. It was unfortunate that she couldn't remember this period for herself, but all the recipes had been recorded in exacting detail, so it wouldn't be too hard to re-create them.

If anything, the problem was whether the people to eat it would have enough time for the meal. The trio was going to be yanked out at five o'clock, whether they liked it or not, so if Kirito got back at 4:55, he was going to have to pack that feast into a five-minute span.

Just make sure you get back with thirty minutes to spare, Asuna thought, speaking to the former Star King, certainly safe and sound on Admina by now. She skipped up the last few steps.

9

Silica and her companions decided to set up a makeshift base just outside the tunnel leading to the wasp dome.

They cleared away the brush, cut down trees, and carved out a flat space about ten yards to the side. Sinon and Klein used their Stoneworking skill to build a foundation, upon which Lisbeth crafted a simple hut with the Carpentry skill. It would easily be shattered upon attack by any large monster, but they only needed it to hold up until they conquered the wasp nest.

The reason for building a base was to stockpile resource items, particularly lumber. There were probably hundreds of those giant wasps, which would attack in coordination over a wide range, so it was quite likely that the classic method of luring out one at a time where they were easier to manage would not work. If they were surrounded by a swarm of wasps, it would make escaping the tunnel harder, so the plan was to erect a simple defensive structure within the dome—proposed by Sinon, who called it a "bunker."

Players weren't allowed to place structures on the ground in the wild in *ALO*, but crafting was possible anywhere in *Unital Ring*, whether in a dungeon or on top of a river, and a simple wall took no more than seconds to set up. If you were used to the commands, it wouldn't be that hard to build a bunker while you were in combat.

The real issue was how long a wooden bunker could withstand a barrage of giant wasp attacks, and the only way to find out was to try it. It would be another hour until a minimum number of members would be around to help tackle the fight.

As an expert in sneaking, Friscoll volunteered to be the messenger to Ruis na Ríg. It wasn't entirely clear how much they could trust him, but if his purpose was to be the first to reach the goal, too, there couldn't be any benefit for him to betray them now.

Silica weighed the different options and possibilities in her head as she fed Pina and Misha. The bear ate plenty of harve meat and some blueberry-like berries they harvested while cutting down bushes, then curled up next to the shack and began to nap. Pina alighted on the massive bear and used it as a bed.

Lisbeth, grinning blissfully, watched the pets sleeping. Then her smile vanished, and she muttered, "When *Unital Ring*'s been beaten, this world will turn back into *ALO* and *GGO* again, right?"

"Um...I suppose so?" Silica replied before she realized what Lisbeth was thinking about. When someone reached the center of this world and *Unital Ring* vanished, Misha, the other pets, and the Bashin and Patter would go with it. Even newborn Yael would not be spared.

The fragility of virtual worlds was well-known to any VRMMO player. While using the Seed Package to build a game lowered the initial costs, it also lowered the resistance to shutting down games faster. In just the last year and a half, dozens of games had been taken offline, and all the NPCs that lived in those worlds had disappeared with them.

But the AI level of the *Unital Ring* NPCs was several levels above any other game's. Every NPC here seemed equipped with the same level of intelligence as only a few special NPCs in *ALO*, like the gods and giants. Even pets like Misha and Kuro didn't just execute a few standard routines, but exhibited the ability to understand complex orders, a sign of having their own AI.

Thousands of natives living in the vast world of *Unital Ring* vanishing in an instant? It was out of their hands, but even still, it seemed cruel. However...

"Even if we're not the ones who beat the game, *someone* will...," Silica said, condensing her thought process into one simple answer.

Lisbeth nodded. "For now, we don't have any option other than heading for the goal."

"Yes. Let's do our best to beat this wasp nest."

They bumped knuckles, right as someone called for them from the other side of the clearing. Silica waved, then trotted over to where Sinon and Klein were waiting.

The four of them focused on collecting resources while they waited for more players to arrive.

They'd need iron nails and sawed boards to make any proper wooden construction, but the bunker only needed to last for the length of the battle, so they made as many logs and ropes as they could, saving them up in the stockpile space within the shack.

Forty minutes later, when they had just about filled up the capacity of the shack, a number of footsteps approached from the southwest. They watched warily, just in case, but the group that emerged through the woods was a party much larger than what they'd expected.

In the lead was Friscoll, wearing a robe that made him look like a bagworm. Behind him were Agil, Argo, and Leafa. Then there were Holgar, Dikkos, and a few more ex-members of Mutasina's army; Zarion, Beeming, and more from *Insectsite*; then three or four each of the Bashin and Patter. The group was nearly twenty strong.

Silica walked over, her caution forgotten, and gave the group an abbreviated greeting before telling Leafa, "I'm amazed you got this many! I know it's Saturday, but it's still early..."

"Well, that's the thing," said Leafa, glancing at Friscoll, who was talking with Agil and Klein about something. "He just went running all through Ruis na Ríg and rounded everyone up. Seems like he even picked up Bashin and Patter language at some point..."

"Guy's gonna put me outta business." Argo scowled. But then she smirked and added, "I was the one who reached out to Zarion's group, though."

"Out of our group, only Agil, Argo, and Asuna have any fluency in English," Leafa noted, which was a fact. Kirito could speak a fair bit, too—he was considering going to school in America, after all—but not to a native extent. Silica was trying her best to study foreign language now, after she'd been totally unable to explain herself to any of the other players in the Otherworld War, since her speaking was very clumsy and she could only understand them if they talked slowly and simply enough for her.

Since they had the *Insectsite* players on their side, she wanted to overcome the intimidation from their appearances and be proactive in communicating, so Silica walked over to where the group was chatting with the Patter.

But before she could say anything, Zarion the rhinoceros beetle turned to her and said, at the very upper limit of the speed she could make out by ear, "Hey, girl, these fluffies are saying they know about the giant hornets we're about to fight."

"Really?" she replied, and turned to the three Patter.

The leader of the trio was Chett. She wore a light-green bandana around her head, neatly designed leather armor, and had a gleaming pitchfork slung over her back. She stood a bit over three feet tall and was a heroic figure who faced the Life Harvester without fear—but now it seemed that her ears and snout were slightly downcast.

"Silica, are you really going to fight the big green wasps?" Chett said, her words crisp and clear thanks to Silica's hard work grinding up the Patter language skill.

"Yes. We must pass through the place where the wasp nest is if we want to go deeper into the forest," Silica replied. The two Patter warriors who stood behind Chett—Chinoki on the right and Chilph on the left, if she recalled correctly—both twitched their whiskers. The swarm of giant wasps was an undeniable threat, but it seemed surprising to Silica that they would be so frightened before they'd even seen the creatures.

"When I was a child, my nana told me that long, long ago, it was terrifying green wasps that drove the Patter off the plains," said Chett before she launched into the history of her people.

In the distant past, the Patter built a magnificent city on a rocky mountain to the north of the Giyoru Savanna. They grew corn, raised honeybees, and lived in peace.

But one day, the earth trembled and shook, and the side of the mountain collapsed. Then a swarm of green wasps, bigger than anything they'd ever seen, appeared and attacked the Patter. Those who fought back and those who ran and hid were killed in equal numbers, and in no time the wasps had control over the city. The survivors escaped to the savanna to the south, where ferocious dinosaurs pushed them farther to the east, until a small handful of just a few dozen reached the Great Wall of Gaiyu.

Since then, the Patter had eked out a meager existence inside the great wall, living in fear of the frogs and lizards inside, dreaming of one day reaching the land of promise to the far east…

The entire group had formed a circle to listen to the story. When Chett finished, her big eyes dripped with tears.

Her reason to cry was quite understandable. They had reached the Great Zelletelio Forest as they'd so dearly desired, only to encounter the same giant wasps that had ruined their old city in its prime. That was surely worthy of despair. It seemed to Silica that they were in danger of having all the Patter decide to move out of Ruis na Ríg to a safer place.

"In that case, Chett, this is the perfect opportunity," said Sinon calmly. She'd been listening quietly next to Silica the entire time.

Chett turned in her direction with surprise, and asked, "Opportunity? For what?"

"For avenging your ancestors. I suppose they might be a different swarm from the ones that destroyed your city, but they're clearly still the same species. Plus, if we figure out how to vanquish them, we might have a chance to take back your city one day. Assuming there's still a nest there."

"Take back our city…," repeated Chett, trying on the words for size. Her drooping ears began to perk up bit by bit. Light returned to her darkened eyes, and her whiskers stood at attention again.

She turned to look at Chinoki and Chilph, then said, surprisingly, "Our ancestors were driven out by the green wasps, but they fought bravely. They learned the wasps' weakness, and the elder told that secret to his children, who told their children, and so on. I am the child of Chignook, our current elder. I know the weakness."

After those who knew Patter filled in the others on what she had said, a murmur of surprise ran through the group.

Most likely, learning how to defeat the giant wasps was supposed to follow these steps: speak to all the NPCs around the Stiss Ruins where the *ALO* players initially spawned, put together the clues to travel to the Great Wall of Gaiyu, then clear some quests to earn the Patter's trust. But because Kirito's group, in the process of finding Sinon, ended up taking the Patter all the way to Ruis na Ríg, the process had been significantly abbreviated. This might be a big chance to catch up to the *Apocalyptic Date* and *Asuka Empire* groups, who supposedly had the lead for now.

Silica stepped forward and asked, "Wh-what is that weakness?"

"Lobelia flowers," stated the brave rat warrior firmly.

10

"Do these flowers have a name?" I asked, picking up one such plant, torn halfway down the stalk.

Lifelessly, Eolyne replied, "They might...but I do not know it."

"Probably a flower that doesn't exist in Cardina," I muttered, gazing at the yellow petals. They looked as delicate as woven silk. Within moments, the flower's life was fully expended, and it vanished from my fingers in a little puff of light.

A curtain of countless particles lifted up from the ground around my feet and melted away into the chilly night breeze. It was the life of all the flowers and bushes that the X'rphan Mk. 13's emergency landing had crushed. The dark gash of the slide mark in the pale-yellow field was a good 150 feet long—and that was with Incarnation working to minimize the momentum. We had probably violated some kind of rule in carving it out, but surely the blame for that could be placed on whoever was firing missiles at the X'rphan.

The problem was who that was—and why we'd been attacked. But the pilot commander, who seemed like he might have an idea, was kneeling at the edge of the scar on the ground, gazing dully at the X'rphan's body. He seemed to be devastated that he'd allowed the legendary Star King's craft to be destroyed.

The damage to the X'rphan Mk. 13 was indeed considerable.

The mysterious bio-missile had come up from below, torn open the craft's armored belly, and severed or cracked several engine pipes within. Strangely, there were no burn marks, and the canisters containing the eternal-heat elements and wind elements were safe. But this was clearly more damage than we could repair with impromptu means.

My gaze rose upward. We had descended on the day side of Admina and flown toward the night side, so the light of sunrise was to our east, but the sky overhead was still dark. In the center of that expanse was a shockingly large blue planet: Cardina.

According to Eolyne, the two planets were about 300,000 miles apart. The X'rphan had crossed that distance in just an hour and a half, which would make its top speed over 180,000 miles per hour—close to Mach 300. Even adding the acceleration of Cardina's rotation, it was a speed that was impossible in real-world planes. From what I recalled, even the escape velocity for rockets leaving Earth was about 25,000 miles per hour.

The fact that the Underworlders, previously having no means of flight aside from dragons, had achieved this technological feat in just two hundred years was astonishing. But it also meant that with the X'rphan damaged, Eolyne and I had lost our means of returning to Cardina. Technically, we could fly back with Incarnation, but I couldn't pull off a speed like 180,000 miles per hour.

Before we got out of the X'rphan, I noted on the dashboard that it was a bit after two o'clock, Cardina time, so we had less than three hours until our time limit with Dr. Koujiro. It was highly questionable if we'd be able to accomplish our goals here in that time, and it would be even harder to return to Asuna and Alice in Central Cathedral. But we certainly weren't going to solve anything by sitting around here.

"Hey, Eolyne," I said. The pilot commander turned to me, revealing his white leather mask. He had already taken off his helmet. I circled around in front of him and put my hands on my knees. "Do you still believe I'm the actual Star King?"

Through the mask, I saw Eolyne blink with surprise. He nodded. "Yes...I do."

"Then in the name of Star King Kirito, I forgive you for damaging the X'rphan. For one thing, it was my fault for not noticing that black worm coming up from below. So let's put an end to the self-pity and start talking about what to do now."

"......"

His mouth fell open in shock and only closed when he was ready to smirk. "I wasn't pitying myself."

"Liar. You were acting just like you did when we got locked in the cells under the cathe—" I caught myself and shook my head. "I mean, never mind. Look, just stand up."

I held out my hand to him, stifling the stab of pain in my chest. Eolyne narrowed his eyes in suspicion, but he took my hand and pulled himself to his feet. I helped brush off some of the leaves on the back of his uniform before turning to the X'rphan.

"We'll have to leave it here. On that note...how come whoever knocked us down isn't attacking?"

After our landing, my first concern was a follow-up attack from whoever had fired the Incarnate-guided projectiles. But over five minutes had passed, and there was only silence in the skies and on the ground.

Eolyne had considered this already; his answer was immediate: "The question is, was that an automated security system that fired those guided missiles, or was it intended to slow us down here on Admina?"

"Automated security system...? Do you have those things, too?"

"The ground force was trying to implement something like that. But they couldn't solve the issue of how to tell apart friend from foe, so the project was shelved, as I recall..."

"Ah, I see."

Naturally, identifying friend and foe in the real world happened through radio signals, but the Underworld didn't have the concept of radio. The vocal transmitters at the Arabel mansion and the imperial villa ran on some property that was completely distinct from cellular phones.

"Meaning it's possible to create a device that can fire a guided projectile at any dragoncraft it detects?"

"...Theoretically," said Eolyne, although it wasn't the most confident answer. "The problem is what was mixed among the guided missiles—what you called a black worm. Is it possible to load something like that in an automated launcher...?"

"Yeah, that's a good question," I agreed.

We looked at the X'rphan's rear. There was a huge chunk of ice on the ground nearby. The surface was coated with dust and dirt, but it was highly transparent, making it easy to see what was trapped inside the ice.

Without a word, we approached the block. Up close, the black worm—the bio-missile—was much ghastlier than I expected. It was three feet long and two inches wide—a long, dark tube, as I'd noticed while we were in combat. But up close, I could see small hexagonal scales all over its surface, and its semitranslucent head had dark spots in a ring pattern, like those parasites that infected a snail's eyestalks. The red light they had when chasing the X'rphan was gone, but we couldn't be sure it was dead.

"...Hey, Eolyne."

"...What is it?"

"What does your family call you?"

"Huh?" the commander exclaimed. "Are you really asking me that right now?"

"When you're having difficult conversations, it helps to abbreviate what you call each other, right? Just call me Kirito."

"......"

Eolyne heaved an elegant, dramatic sigh that made patently clear his doubts that he was talking to the *real* Star King. "Mom... my mother called me Eo or Eol."

"All right. May I call you Eo, too?"

"Go ahead," he said, waving his hand ostentatiously.

I cleared my throat. "*Ahem*...So, Eo, have you ever seen any-thing like this before?"

"No. But..."

Eolyne hesitated, then reached out to touch the block of ice that he had created. Then he swiftly pulled back his hand, as though the ice had caused him pain.

"...There is an ancient text that contains a particular passage. This black worm reminds me of it."

"Text...?"

"It's a detailed record of the Otherworld War, a document that only members of the Stellar Unification Council can view. At the end of the Battle of the Eastern Gate, the Dark Territory's sorcerers used a forbidden art that converted the life of their fellow soldiers directly into spatial resources, fashioning them into living weapons with the capability to follow targets of their own accord. I believe they were called...deathworms..."

"...Deathworms," I repeated, feeling the skin on my arms prickle, the hairs standing on end.

While I was still in a comatose state during that battle, under the protection of Ronie and Tiese, I was able to vaguely sense the events transpiring around me.

A separate troop of human soldiers charging through the pass was set upon by a dark-element art resembling a mass of starving insects. It was a single Integrity Knight, calling all of that magic onto himself, who gave his life to protect his people.

After the battle, I learned that this knight was Eldrie Synthesis Thirty-One, whom I'd crossed swords with in the Rose Garden of Central Cathedral. His mentor, Alice, still kept his divine weapon, the Frostscale Whip, safe and sound in storage.

A horrifying magical weapon of slaughter from the war two centuries ago, used today...and on the surface of Admina?

Eolyne could sense my skepticism. "I agree, it doesn't seem possible. The large-scale offensive arts used in the Otherworld War were all supposed to be destroyed after the war was finished. But of course...any sorcerer who was able to incant the arts would naturally have the formula memorized…so there is always the possibility that it was secretly written down and saved somewhere."

"Yes…that's true."

Sacred arts formulas, all starting with the phrase "System Call," were something like a primitive form of spoken computer programming. If you understood the meaning of the words being used, you didn't need to memorize or write down anything, and it was easy to alter them. It would probably take time to modify the deathworm art to create this black worm, but a skilled sorcerer could probably do it.

But we didn't have time to dig into the details of that now.

"So…what do we do with this worm?" I asked.

Eolyne murmured to himself, thinking hard, then suggested, "If the ice melts, it might start moving again. But I wouldn't want to damage it and cause an explosion, either. Can you do something with your Incarnation, Kirito?"

"Um…are you sure I'm allowed to do that?"

"You used it when trying to stop the guided missiles and when the X'rphan landed, so there's no point trying to pretend that didn't happen. Of course, the smaller the effect, the better."

"I don't know if I can do smaller…"

Manipulating things with Incarnation required more imagination the further your intended effect differed from the common sense of the world. Even to do something relatively simple and mundane like burning things, it took more Incarnation to do to stone or metal than something readily flammable like paper or wood.

If I thought my hardest, I could possibly eliminate the entire block of ice, worm and all. But to do it on a smaller scale, as Eolyne requested, I'd need to use a means that was more in-line with the properties of the worm.

"Hmm…"

I pressed against the ice block with my hand. Using the tiniest bit of Incarnation like a 3D scanner, I tried touching the black worm. I expected to be blocked by that Incarnation-violating substance, but it seemed to have vanished along with the red light.

The first thing I felt was the sensation of cold. Not from myself, but the still-living black worm, which desired warmth. Whoever had created this imitation life-form had instilled a primordial fear of cold into the worm, programming it to seek out the nearest source of warmth—such as a dragoncraft's eternal-heat element.

I continued scanning. In the belly of the worm were four dark elements. They would probably burst if they approached a heat element. In other words, it wasn't a simple explosion that ripped over the X'rphan's armor, but a micro black hole without heat of its own.

It was too dangerous to do anything with the black worm without taking care of the dark elements first. I thought for a bit, then stuck out my left hand, keeping the right busy with the Incarnation scan.

"Gimme a light element, Eo."

"...Give you one? You can't make your own?" he grumbled, but stuck his index finger over my palm and silently generated a pale glowing dot. I took it and pressed my palm against the block of ice.

Light elements would bounce off mirrors but pass through any translucent material. Since the frost-element-derived ice block Eolyne made had essentially zero impurities, the mote of light sank into it without any resistance. I created the tiniest hole in the black worm's body and slipped the light element inside it.

A purple light blinked and went out. The dark and light elements, as opposing forces, had canceled each other out.

After repeating that process three more times, the dark elements within the black worm were all gone, and I was able to exhale with relief. There was no longer any danger of it turning into a mini black hole, but the worm itself was still alive, and its drive to find heat was unaffected. If we let it out of the ice, it might still wriggle its way into the damaged craft's insides and jam itself into a pipe or something, even if it didn't explode.

"Hmm…"

After some more thought, I decided to scan the worm's body a second time.

I found that, in addition to the translucent head, I could also sense something like a faint consciousness from the body, even after the dark elements were removed. When I saw the stripes on its head, I felt it was like a parasite, and it seemed there really was a different creature occupying the head, the one that was seeking out heat. That was probably the source of the substance that melted my Incarnate wall, too.

Pressing all my fingers against the ice, I cut open the black worm's head with an Incarnate scalpel and carefully extracted the exposed parasite.

"Eugh. What are you doing, Kirito?" said Eolyne with undisguised disgust. I appreciated that he was finally being a bit more casual around me, but I was too busy concentrating to respond.

The elliptical parasite had a narrow tube running from its end into the black worm's body. Very carefully, I pulled it out, trying not to rip it.

Eventually, the entirety of the tube was free, and the two pieces were totally separate—at which point the parasite visibly began to shrivel inside the ice. Apparently, it could not survive on its own. In just seconds, it had lost its shape and melted into yellow liquid.

"…I think that's removed the danger," I said, the tension in my shoulders easing at last.

The pilot commander did not approach, however. "It's still alive, isn't it?"

"Yes, it is…but it'll probably die if I crushed the whole ice block."

"Ugh…I don't really want to watch that…"

"I don't want to do it, either." I grimaced. I was about to lower my hand when I picked up another very faint signal of desire.

The body of the black worm, separated from the parasite, was still exuding some kind of instinctual impulse. It was seeking…

heat? No, not that. It wasn't a simple heat source, but a more abstract kind of warmth.

The instant I realized what it was, I gasped.

"...What is it, Kirito?" Eolyne whispered.

I mumbled, "It's a child...a baby."

"A b-baby?"

"It's a newborn. Whoever created this fed dark elements to a baby, stuck another creature into its head, and fashioned it into a guided missile."

Eolyne seemed hesitant, unsure of what he was hearing in my tone of voice. Quietly, he asked, "Kirito...are you sympathizing with it?"

"No, not really...I'm angry at whoever created it."

"I think that's the same thing..."

I ignored his comment and pressed my hands to the block of ice again.

The black worm was a man-made creature of darkness. Unlike ordinary living things, sacred arts made with light elements would not restore its life. But if I sent dark elements in to touch it, they would harm its body because of the way they ate away at solid material.

Fortunately, cold ice was closer to dark than light, in terms of the elements. Concentrating hard, I converted the water in the center of the ice block to a mist-form dark element. The required intensity of Incarnation to do this was much, much lower than creating darkness from fire.

When he saw the black worm surrounded by purple mist, Eolyne murmured, "Oh...you can perform matter conversion without any spoken words? No wonder you're a legend..."

"Enough about that. Trust me—my conversion abilities are nothing compared to the great and mighty pontifex," I replied, then realized that it was the first time I'd ever spoken about Administrator of the Axiom Church in Eolyne's presence. The commander seemed only mildly quizzical, however, and did not say anything about it.

I returned my focus to the block of ice. As I expected, the black worm absorbed the dark-type mist all over its body, which restored its life.

Even the cut on the worm's head, which I made to remove the parasite, was healing, and a new organ was growing in. Three little orbs on each side shone like rubies. They were probably eyes. There was no mouth, but in combination with the scales covering its body, it was starting to look more like a snake than an earthworm. This was probably its original form before it had been modified into a weapon.

The black worm, now a black snake, began to wriggle inside the little cavity within the ice block. It pressed the tip of its head against the walls here and there, searching for an exit.

"...What are you going to do?" Eolyne asked.

"I think if I release it, it's going to return to where it was born," I explained.

"Ah...I see." His eyes were sharp behind the mask. "And if we follow it, we might find out who made it...or failing that, the whereabouts of the production facility. Seems like a good plan to me..."

"The problem is what we'll do if it starts flying with the same speed as the guided missiles," I said preemptively, and tapped the ground with my foot. "I guess we'll just have to tough it out and run. Are you good at running long-distance, Eo?"

"I'm not bad at it, but I don't like it, either."

"Neither do I. Well, let's set it loose..."

I glanced at the sky to the east. The orange of the coming sunrise was spreading over the gentle hills ahead. Once the sun rose, the dark gouges in the yellow flower field from our crash and the silvery X'rphan Mk. 13 itself would stand out.

First, I reached toward the skid marks and summoned a mental image. From within the exposed earth, countless tiny buds appeared. They grew larger by the moment, spread leaves, added buds, and then bloomed into brilliant flowers.

Once I was satisfied that the marks were gone, I pointed my

hand at the damaged craft. I chose to focus only on the vine-based flowers out of the many that were present, causing them to fuse and grow over the body of the ship. When the vines completely covered the craft from nose to tail wings, I made them bloom, and then the massive dragoncraft looked like nothing but a small flower-covered hill.

"...It's just like the story of Hoyer the Flower Summoner," Eolyne commented. I frowned, but eventually said, "Uh, sure." I'd never heard of such a story before in my life, but if I started asking, the sun would rise before I finished.

But I'd covered what needed to be hidden, so I turned back to the ice block. The trapped black snake was moving more frantically than before. Just in case, I focused on its mind again, but I didn't sense any hostility toward us.

"Okay, I'm going to break the ice," I announced. The pilot commander nodded.

We were both wearing our leather pilot uniforms, but the air was cool here, so I didn't see any trouble with running in it. If anything, I was more concerned with the weight of the Night-Sky Blade and Blue Rose Sword on my waist—and I certainly couldn't leave them behind.

If I needed to, I could use Incarnation to cheat on the weight, I told myself, and drew the Night-Sky Blade.

It wasn't clear how many years had passed since the Star King last used this sword, but there wasn't so much as a smudge on the black blade. I hadn't had the frame of mind to think about my sword when I used it on the door unlocking mechanism of the cathedral's eightieth floor, so I took the time now to think, *Here we go again, partner*, and pressed the tip against the top of the ice block.

"......!"

With just the tiniest pressure, the block cracked loudly.

The huge mass of ice silently split into left and right. The sides of the cut were as smooth as mirrors and glowed orange with the light of the morning rays.

The moment the two pieces of ice fell to the ground, the black snake began to float up into the air in its freedom. I had no idea how it was actually flying, but its wounds seemed to be totally healed.

Three red eyes looked down at me and Eolyne. But it turned its head away without much interest and flew into the darkened western sky.

"Let's follow it!" I called out, sliding the Night-Sky Blade back into its sheath. I started running, and Eolyne rushed to follow.

Fortunately, the speed of the black snake as it undulated through the sky was far slower than when it was a missile. Even still, if I had to run at my very fastest, I wouldn't last a single minute in the real world. There was stress upon my body in the Underworld, too, of course, but your longevity here was tied to your object control authority number. Eolyne's authority level was 62, if I remembered correctly, a number even higher than the old Integrity Knights', so he wouldn't tire easily. I didn't even feel like taking my 129 number seriously.

"Just say something if you're getting tired, Eo!" I called out just in case.

"Same goes for you, Kirito!" he replied, more than game.

His tone of voice was so reminiscent of my late friend that I nearly gasped, and I briefly lost my pace. But I gritted my teeth and pushed harder. I managed to stabilize my posture, and looked into the navy-blue sky.

Ten yards ahead, the black snake was so dark that if I lost my focus for even a second, I might lose sight of it against the gloom. I had a goal to achieve right now, and I needed to use every ounce of my power to do it. For Alice if for nothing else, while she waited on Cardina to be reunited with Selka.

My mindset renewed, I picked up the pace a little bit more.

11

"Lobelia flowers..."

After some consideration, Sinon concluded that she had no memory of any items by that name.

But before she could ask Chett for more details, Silica and Lisbeth both cried, "Lobelia?!"

"Wait, you know it?" Sinon asked. They nodded, but their faces were grim with fear and alarm.

"...It's an ingredient for a level-5 paralysis and damage poison," Silica said in a quiet rasp.

"Is that...in *ALO*?" Sinon asked.

"No. Not *ALO*," said Lisbeth, shaking her head. All eyes trained on her. Her answer took them all by surprise. "Lobelia flowers were from *SAO*."

Why would a poisonous flower from the world of *Sword Art Online*, which had been gone for nearly two years, exist in the world of *Unital Ring*? That mystery would have to wait. They asked Chett for more information.

She said that lobelia, the necessary item to defeat the giant green wasps, grew at the base of old, dead trees. For one thing, there were no trees on the arid Giyoru Savanna, and any trees that did die would crumble away within moments, so the Patter's ancestors had been unable to gather enough to stop the giant wasps. But there were tons and tons of trees in the Great Zelletelio Forest, and the dead trees would not just vanish. There were, in fact, dead trees devoid of leaves here and there throughout the forest wherever they walked.

If they had known this was the case, they would have been gathering lobelia flowers from such trees all along, but this was just how RPGs worked. On top of that, they didn't know what the flowers looked like. Chett had never seen lobelia flowers for herself, so originally they would have needed to go by the description her father had told her. But because Lisbeth, Silica, Argo, Klein, and Agil had been in *SAO*, they had seen the real plant in Aincrad.

The five *SAO* players spread out to look for large dead trees. Agil was the first to raise his hand and call out, "Found some!" The others gathered around him.

The ax warrior pointed out a tiny flower hidden at the foot of a decaying tree. Its four petals were a beautiful violet blue, but the way its stalk twisted as though in agony was a bit creepy. The leaves were a purplish green, and the pistil and stamen were black.

"Aww, it's so cute. It doesn't look violently poisonous at all," opined Dikkos, the leader of the Weed Eaters. He crouched down toward the flower, his scale armor clinking loudly, and reached for it.

"Ah!" exclaimed Silica and Agil, but it was too late. He grabbed the base of the lobelia stalk with his bare fingers and pulled it loose.

"Hgyaaaah!" Dikkos screamed immediately, arching his back. Then he toppled to the ground on his left side. His HP bar was now accompanied by an icon of a blue flower on a black background. Dikkos was frozen still, and his HP was slowly decreasing, meaning the Debuff was doing both paralysis and damage.

"C'mon, pal, don't pluck it with yer bare hand!" exclaimed Argo with exasperation. She took a little bottle from her belt pouch, pulled out the stopper, and stuck it in Dikkos's mouth. It was an antidote potion that Asuna and Sinon had made with the Pharmaceutical skill, but it was made with random leaves and nuts found nearby and low skill proficiency. If this didn't work, Dikkos's adventure in *Unital Ring* might be about to end.

Fortunately, however, his HP stopped falling after a third or so, and the Debuff icon vanished shortly thereafter. Dikkos sat up unsteadily, moved away from the nearby lobelia flower, and groaned, "Man, that one got me good…I thought the Antivenom and Resistance abilities would help me, but even still, it hit me with a poison status just from plucking it."

"We warned you it was really dangerous. If you had eaten it, you'd be dead by now," Lisbeth scolded him.

Wistfully, Chett added, "I thought all humans were smart."

Despite the unnecessary trouble, everyone had the chance to see what a lobelia looked like, so from that point on, they were able to split into groups of three or four to search and harvest the plants.

At three o'clock, they came back together and tossed their flowers into a large stew pot Klein pulled from his inventory. Despite twenty people searching over a wide area, they didn't have enough to fill even half the pot. Luckily, Chett told them it was enough.

They set up a hearth and table in front of their storage hut, filled the pot with enough water to soak all the lobelia flowers, then started a low fire beneath it. It started steaming almost instantly, so Sinon quietly asked Chett, "Is it safe to breathe in this steam?"

"It is fine. But Daddy said to never, ever taste the broth."

"I wasn't planning to," Sinon said with a smirk, and leaned over the pot. Instantly, her nostrils were full of a smell like nothing of this world—though technically, a virtual world was not "of this world." The pleasant scent filled her head and left her in a momentary daze.

It was a scent that was sweet and fresh and rich all at once; she imagined that high-end perfumes costing tens of thousands of yen a bottle probably smelled like this, not that she had ever used one. At some point, Silica, Lisbeth, and Leafa had gathered around the pot, breathing it in deeply.

Sinon made sure to get another lungful to enjoy, then exhaled. "I see...No wonder they have to warn people not to taste it."

"I know what you mean. It smells so sweet," Silica agreed.

At some point, the pot's contents had turned the same bright blue as the flower petals. The flowers themselves had wilted, soon to dissolve altogether, it seemed.

Simply plucking one of these flowers barehanded was enough to be nearly fatal, so what kind of poison would you get by boiling an entire pot of them? If someone were to grab the pot and slosh it over everyone here, it would probably be enough to kill every last person in the group. The thought made Sinon shiver.

"...If we can make this poison, then other groups could, too...like Mutasina's forces," she murmured. The others nodded, considering the same point. Even aloof Klein was grimacing like he'd eaten something bitter.

"The PKers used plenty of poisons in *SAO*, too," he noted. "If this really is a level-5 poison, it's pretty scary that you can craft it already at this point..."

"We gotta develop an antidote to this stuff quick, too," Argo added.

Chett's thin tail swung back and forth. "Lobelia poison is scary, but it's not scary."

"Wh-what does that mean?" asked Lisbeth.

The Patter's little body leaned back as far as it could comfortably go. "Thirty minutes after it is finished, this poison's color and smell will leach out. Then it becomes water again."

"......"

The group shared a look. If its efficacy as a poison lasted only half an hour, it would be difficult to use in a large-scale PK attack. But that also meant they needed to start the assault—no, finish—against the wasps within that time frame.

"Chett, how many more minutes until it's ready?" Sinon asked.

The Patter girl peered into the pot and frowned. "Once all the flowers have melted. Probably about five minutes."

"Hey, we can't sit back on our haunches, then," said Klein. He, Agil, and Argo rushed around to the other members of the group chatting in the area to explain the situation. Sinon, Silica, and Lisbeth arranged little pottery jars on the table and prepared to portion out the poison.

It was impossible to say if their improvised plan would work on the first try. There was a decent chance something unexpected would throw a wrench into whatever plan they had, as with the battle against Mutasina last night. But the strength of VRMMO players was in considering all the different possibilities and stubbornly developing contingency plans. Sinon had learned that from Kirito, and so had the others. No matter how muddy and wretched, whoever survived to the end was the winner. It was the case in *GGO*'s Bullet of Bullets, and it was true here in *Unital Ring*, too.

Sinon looked up at the hazy sky, thought about Kirito, Asuna, and Alice, who were off fighting under a different sky entirely, and thought, *We're doing our best over here, too.*

12

At no point, in either the real world or any virtual world, had I ever run as hard as I was now, I decided as I sprinted pell-mell after the flying black snake.

Fortunately, the landscape itself was completely consistent in its series of low, rolling hills, and my well of stamina was deeper than I'd realized. My breath got ragged and my muscles burned, but I was maintaining a pace that would have left me collapsed long ago in the real world, and Eolyne was keeping up.

I recalled that during the Otherworld War two centuries ago, the human army's secondary force and the Dark Territory's pugilists guild traveled hundreds of miles on foot. My authority level was far higher than theirs, so I couldn't possibly give up and cry uncle after a few dozen miles, I scolded myself.

After thirty minutes of sprinting, the black snake finally began to drift downward. Inwardly praying, I said, "Are we finally reaching the goal?"

"I can only hope so," said Eolyne. I looked over my shoulder at him.

His Highness the pilot commander had loosened his uniform down to the chest, and sweat ran down his forehead. The leather mask looked extremely uncomfortable, and if I wasn't so self-conscious about bringing it up, I would have told him to just take it off.

Then again, he had said he wore the mask because the skin around his eyes was sensitive to sunlight. Solus still hadn't risen over the slopes to the east, so he should probably be able to remove it now, at least for a little bit.

"Oh! Kirito, there!" Eolyne cried, pulling my attention away from him.

There was something beyond the hill we were climbing now.

At the foot of a basin collecting the predawn darkness, there was an obviously man-made structure. It was about the height of a three-story building, and not that wide, either, but it was accompanied by a nearby road about five hundred yards long—no, a runway. Making this...

"...A base?"

"So it seems," Eolyne agreed. He put a hand on my shoulder to hold me back, then proceeded to the top of the hill, staying low, and finally getting down to a crawl.

In the sky, the black snake was flying right at the rectangular building, until it was no longer visible among the shadow. That told me it was almost certain that whatever had birthed that black snake was inside the building.

"Kirito, can you see that? Beyond the runway," Eolyne whispered suddenly. I looked to the left.

At the end of the runway huddled something dark. At first I took it for some kind of massive ray, until I understood that this, too, was man-made. It was an enormous dragoncraft, even larger than the X'rphan Mk. 13.

"...Those wings are enormous...," I murmured back.

"Yes," Eolyne agreed, "it's been maximized for capacity, not speed. There are a bunch of supports under those huge main wings, I believe."

"Meaning...that's what shot all those guided missiles at us?"

"I think so," he replied quietly. "But if so, it means we were detected approaching Admina ahead of time. Either our information leaked somehow or they're utilizing some kind of advanced detection system that even I don't know about..."

I was a total amateur when it came to military and intelligence matters, of course, but I understood that either of these cases was a big deal to Eolyne. I couldn't just shrug it off as "not my problem," but I didn't have anything to add.

"...Kirito. I have to investigate that base. Of course, it'll involve some level of danger, so I can't ask you to come with me..."

"Of course I will. It shouldn't be a question," I hastened to reply. Before Eolyne could protest, I added, "If I let you go alone and anything happens, I don't know what I'll say to Stica and Laurannei. Plus, maybe what I'm looking for is in there. In fact... if it's okay to use Incarnation, we don't need to sneak. I can just pull that building up out of the ground and take the walls and roof off piece by piece..."

"......"

Whether out of annoyance or admiration—surely the former—Eolyne said nothing for several seconds. He recovered and shook his head. "No. The people in there might know we crash-landed, but they shouldn't know we've found their base yet. The perpetrator might be somewhere else right now, and there's no harm in maintaining our secrecy for the time being."

"That's a good point...All right, I'll follow your orders from here on," I announced. While Eolyne shot me a suspicious look, he accepted the offer.

"Very well. I only have one order, though: Hold my hand and don't let go."

"H-hold your hand...? I don't think we're at the age where we need to worry about getting lost."

"That's not what I mean. We have to use Hollow Incarnation."

"H-holo...?"

I couldn't process what word he had said and had to wait for Eolyne to trace the spelling in the air for me.

"Hollow...? What do you mean?"

"It's the advanced form of the Incarnation-Hiding Incarnation I mentioned earlier: Incarnation that removes your existence."

"Removes your...existence..."

It was my turn to be totally shaken. I stared at the white leather mask, aghast, and asked him quietly, "Do you mean imagining yourself being obliterated?"

"No, not like that," Eolyne said, shaking his head forcefully. In a warning tone, he explained, "It's held to be impossible to remove yourself from existence with the power of Incarnation. After all, the source of the Incarnation is yourself. It would be like trying to use the suction tube of a cleaning machine to suck up the machine itself."

Huh! So they have something like a vacuum cleaner here, too? I thought, getting distracted. "That's a good point," I said out loud.

Eolyne's mouth was still pursed. "But with the level of Incarnation you can wield, I suppose you might twist that law of nature, too, Kirito. So don't attempt to erase yourself with Incarnation, even as a joke."

"I-I'll take that lesson to heart," I swore, raising my hand. "But then what is this Hollow Incarnation?"

"To put it simply, it's using Incarnation to erase yourself from another person's perception...Well, maybe *erase* isn't the right word...Diluting? Fusing, maybe..."

"Diluting? Fusing...?" I repeated.

On his stomach on the ground, Eolyne shrugged. "It'd take me an hour to attempt to explain with any detail. Just trust that if you stick with me, the guards won't spot you."

"A-all right...I believe you."

"Good. Then take my hand," he said, offering his left. I grabbed it and held tight.

Eolyne's eyes shut, and he let out a long, slow breath.

I was suddenly overtaken by a very strange sensation. A kind of rippling effect took place before my eyes, starting in front of me and spreading behind. The boundary between me and the world became vague, and a weightless feeling took hold in me, as though my flesh were expanding into air.

The feeling dulled very quickly but did not disappear altogether. *Diluting* was indeed a good word for it. My very existence was thinner than before.

Next to me, the contours of Eolyne's figure were subtly but undeniably wavering. It felt like we had both become ghosts. I squeezed without thinking, and he squeezed back as a sign of reassurance. The thinning effect was only visual. Our bodies still occupied the space.

If this truly odd sensation was an effect of manipulating reality through imagination, then Eolyne's Incarnation might not match mine in terms of simple strength, but his technique far outclassed mine.

I shouldn't be getting full of myself just because I can do things like create defensive walls and lift dragoncraft into the air, I scolded myself. We started walking down the hill, matching our steps carefully.

The mysterious base was far more elaborate than I took it for at first.

The building itself was a sturdy mix of metal framework and stone; the walls seemed to be nearly three feet thick. Despite my confident comments earlier, it would hardly be a walk in the park to lift something like this with Incarnation alone.

It looked to be about fifty yards to a side and ten yards tall. The west side, which faced the runway, featured a massive warehouse-style shutter gate, while the personnel entrance was on the south side. We were heading for the back gate on the north side, however.

Guards dressed in dark uniforms stood on either side of the gate. They were holding not swords or spears but what clearly looked like guns. They weren't quite like real-world rifles, but they would do more than hurt if we got shot.

But Eolyne headed directly for the gate, not bothering to even slow down. The guards should be able to see us by now, but neither one was so much as budging.

At the bottom of the hill, the ground turned from flower field to a gravel surface. Our boots made an unpleasant scraping sound, much to my consternation, but the guards did not react to this, either. If Eolyne's Hollow Incarnation were merely an invisibility cloak, it shouldn't cover up our footsteps on top of that, so it seemed that his explanation was accurate: It really did remove our existence from the guards' ability to perceive us at all.

That made me worry about his longevity in maintaining this state, but at this point, all I could do was trust in him. I matched Eolyne's pace as we took the shortest and straightest route to the back door of the base.

Fortunately, the gate was open. If we were preventing the guards from perceiving us, then maybe we could have just flung the gate open without drawing any notice, but I hadn't wanted to test that hypothesis.

The gravel transitioned into paved stone tiles. The blank looks on the guards' faces and their dark, shining rifles were crisp and clear now.

Thinking back on my time in Centoria as a student at Swordcraft Academy, there had never been standing guards like this, and that had been because Underworlders never broke any rules. If a place was labeled off-limits, you didn't need a guard there because no one would ever go inside. The fundamental laws behind that were still intact two centuries later, so why were this base and Central Cathedral guarded so tightly?

I wanted to ask Eolyne this question—he was right next to me. But I'd forgotten to ask if I could speak to him while the Hollow Incarnation was active. It would be a disaster if I caused his Incarnation to waver and the guards spotted us. So I shelved my question for now—which meant there was a good chance I'd forget it later—and focused on walking instead.

The gate was at the end of a fence that jutted out from the side of the building in a rectangular shape. Because it was the rear gate, it was only ten feet or so across. Meaning that, as we were walking side by side, we would be going directly past the guards. I'd experienced this a number of times in *SAO* and *ALO*, but unlike those situations, this was not a quest running on a script. It could turn out the guards were just pretending not to notice us so they could blast us with their guns when we were right next to them.

Keeping myself wary and prepared to deploy an Incarnate shield at the shortest possible warning, I made my way down the last few yards. The eyes of the guards in the fierce helmets turned our way, passed through us, and then traveled back. I felt sweat blossom on my palms, but Eolyne's stayed dry, and the cool texture helped keep me calm and centered.

Eugeo's hands were like this, too.

We passed by the guards and got inside the fence. There were no further guards posted at the back door of the building itself. We quietly opened the glass door and went inside, where a dimly lit hallway continued straight ahead. There was no guard station or reception counter, making it obvious this was not an official facility in any capacity.

Down the corridor, a stairwell appeared on the right. You could go up or down—or continue down the hall. I didn't have time to make a decision before Eolyne pulled me into the stairwell. When we were against the wall, he let go of my hand with a heavy sigh.

Immediately, the wavering of my vision cleared, and the strangely distant sensations vanished. The Hollow Incarnation had been released.

Eolyne's chest was heaving for breath. I asked quietly, "You all right, Eo?"

"…Yes, I'm fine. I'll be better soon."

But despite his reassurance, he was clearly pale even in the dim hallway light. I felt around my uniform belt and pulled a metal bottle off a trio of loops. Laurannei had called it a high-concentration recovery solution. I pulled off the cap and offered it to Eolyne.

The exhaustion that accompanied the use of Incarnation was not a numerical decrease to life but the consumption of the fluctlight—the soul itself—so I didn't know if a healing solution would help. Eolyne took it anyway and thanked me for it.

He put the little bottle to his lips and swallowed it all in one go. When his face was level again, there was an odd expression there, so I asked, "Is it, uh…not very good?"

"It tastes like…dark-roasted cofil tea that was used to pickle siral peel…"

"Uh-huh."

So a rich lemon coffee, then, I thought.

There were no guidance signs in the stairwell, so it wasn't clear what sort of facilities were located on which floors.

"…So where should we start?"

"Where do you think?" he asked in return.

Taken aback, I said, "Well, the basement, I guess."

"Why?"

"Because whenever you're running sketchy tests, you always do it in the basement," I replied.

I recalled then that the only thing below Central Cathedral was cells. But that was a factor of the self-centered, utterly willful ways of Her Holiness Administrator. If the people who shot down the X'rphan were bad guys with more common sense, they would hide whatever things they didn't want seen in the basement level.

Eolyne accepted my simplistic answer and pulled away from the wall.

"Well, let's start from the basement, then. There won't be any Hollow Incarnation from this point on, so make sure you watch our back."

"Got it," I replied, and we began to sneak down the stairs.

13

The finished lobelia poison filled exactly twenty little bottles.

It was lethal enough that a single sip would kill, so they had enough to kill over a hundred players, but the massive green wasps seemed rather poison-resistant, and they weren't just going to drink the substance on command.

Belatedly, Silica began to wonder how they were going to administer the poison to the insects. Thankfully, the Patter ancestors had already solved this in a most unorthodox way.

According to Chett, the giant wasps attacked the towns of large animals like humans and demi-humans, where much prey gathered in one place, and raised huge flowers in the soil where the corpses lay. The nectar of those flowers was the food they used to grow their numbers, so a large group could split off from the colony and start a new one.

There were many rafflesia-like flowers inside the dome they had seen. That meant it was once the home of some kind of animal until the wasps invaded and wiped them out to grow flowers in their place.

"...Meaning if the nest gets too big, some of the wasps will leave to build a new one...," Silica muttered.

Klein added helpfully, "That process is called swarming!"

"Thanks, but we don't need random animal facts right now,"

Lisbeth said without missing a beat. Her lips pressed into a tight line. "If that's true, then they might attack Ruis na Ríg next. That's another reason we don't have time to waste. And with the durability of the poison being very limited, we need to make this snappy."

"That's right. Is everyone ready?" asked Sinon, who was taking on the role of raid leader. The group cheered.

They had handled all the other preparations while the lobelia were stewing. Twenty-four players were taking part in the battle. They split into six parties of between three and five members, with each party receiving three bottles of poison. The last two bottles went to Argo and Chett as backup because of their quickness.

The logs they'd saved up in the hut went to the inventory space of all the strength-based players. The group shared food and drink to ensure everyone's SP and TP were topped off, and morale was high. Now the only thing to do was pray that the Patter's traditional method of killing the giant wasps actually worked.

At three thirty in the afternoon, the group went back through the tunnel and slipped into the dome under the giant tree's branches. According to Friscoll, the rocks and bushes around the dome entrance were outside the wasps' reaction zone, so they built a log wall along that line to serve as a bridgehead. Next, six scout-type players who excelled in stealth slipped into the wasps' activity area, wearing ghillie suits they'd crafted after the Patter's.

The goal was to pour the lobelia poison into the nectar-filled reservoir center of the dozens of rafflesia-like flowers—properly known as gargamols. The wasps would be drawn by the sweet scent, extract some of the poisoned nectar, and suffer its paralysis.

If it worked, it would decrease the enemy's fighting power quite a bit, but the players pouring the poison assumed a lot of risk. The ghillie suits weren't flawless, so if the wasps happened to spot anyone, and they couldn't get back to the bridgehead, they might end up dead.

The volunteers for that dangerous mission were Dikkos, who had surprisingly taken the Swiftness ability, a tiger-beetle Six named Ceecee, Friscoll, Argo, Silica, and Chett the Patter.

Exposing an NPC to mortal danger wasn't ideal, but Chett was absolutely insistent that she take part. She had shown the group how to look for the lobelia flowers, how to extract and use the poison, and even how to make the ghillie suits, so they owed her the right to take part in the mission if that was what she wanted.

Silica whispered to Sinon to provide backup with her gun if Chett needed it, then followed Argo beyond the bridgehead.

She had leveled-up to level-17 while exploring the forest, so her total ability points at the moment were sixteen. She'd saved half of them so far, and used them now on Concealment, a tier-four ability in the Swiftness tree. That would give her Hiding skill a major boost—but unlike in older, traditional games, VRMMOs always had the danger of slipping in muck or tripping over a rock. She warned herself not to be so focused on the air above that she got careless and stumbled over something on the ground.

Silica's assignment was the nine o'clock area, if you viewed the dome like a clock from above and split it into six slices. There were tall bunches of grass here and there along the route, so she waited for an opening when no wasps were around and snuck from bunch to bunch.

The natural dome was fifty yards across, so it wasn't even twenty yards from the waiting area behind the bridgehead to her zone. She reached a large clump of tall grass about halfway down her route in ninety seconds, took a short breather, and checked on the others. Ceecee and Argo chose to do the two farthest spots, and they were already reaching the middle of the dome.

Silica had only ever heard of a tiger beetle by name. It was apparently from Australia and was said to be the fastest land-running insect in the world. In keeping with that reputation, Ceecee's long, skinny legs worked rapidly, zipping from cover to cover like a teleportation spell. Argo, meanwhile, slid along the ground as smoothly as a ninja.

Determined not to be the last to reach her spot, Silica was about to bolt out of the grass when she heard the loud, low buzz of heavy wings just overhead.

Instantly, she froze. Her body was one with the grass, and she thought, *Go away! Get!* But the buzzing only went back and forth and didn't leave her position.

If it had spotted her hiding, it would have attacked by now. She'd have to turn her face upward to learn what was happening, but that would be pointless if it caused the wasp to detect her.

Pina was waiting behind the bridgehead with Misha, and she wasn't equipped with any weapons or armor that would stick out from under the ghillie suit. What was it that was drawing the wasp's attention?

Suddenly, she could hear something scraping near her left shoulder.

Staying in position, she reached over with her right hand to search for the source of the sound. Her fingers brushed a round mass, so she grabbed it and pulled it off her shoulder so she could see it for herself.

"_____!!"

A silent scream ripped out of her throat; it took all her will-power not to allow it to take form.

Scrabbling and working its legs in her hand was a gigantic bug about four inches long. Of course, it wasn't *gigantic* compared to the monstrous wasp hovering overhead, but it was certainly horrendous by real-world standards. The body was as round as a ball and translucent, with golden liquid packed inside. The head was long and narrow, with a protruding needle-type mouth. It probably stabbed plants to suck out the sap, but there was no reason it couldn't do the same with animal blood.

Grabbing it must have counted as an attack, because the game displayed the title *Amber Honeysucker Tick* on a cursor above the insect's head. So it was a tick, not a bug—but that only made it seem 30 percent *more* disgusting, not less. If the tick was the reason the giant wasp was hovering overhead, though…

"...!"

With nothing more than the flick of her wrist, Silica hurled the amber-colored tick to the left. The rounded bug, full with nectar, skittered and rolled along the ground.

Suddenly, the green wasp descended with an especially large buzz. It cradled the tick in its six legs, then flew upward. It had been after the honeysucker tick the whole time. If she hadn't noticed when she did, it might have come right down on top of Silica and spotted her through the disguise.

Looking around with a bit more attention this time, she noticed similar ticks walking here and there across the dome basin. They were probably traps intended for the players trying to steal their way across the dome. If you didn't notice the ticks wandering onto your body, the wasps would come to grab the ticks and spot you.

She wanted to warn the other five players but couldn't shout about it. She could send a player message, but Chett wouldn't get one.

But our companions are all experienced, veteran players, and Chett is a brave, clever warrior. As long as they notice the ticks, they'll figure out the danger they pose, Silica told herself. She resumed her trip, careful not only of wings overhead but also of ticks on the ground. She made it across the remaining ten yards to her objective zone.

There were six gargamol flowers in this area. She had three bottles of lobelia poison, so she could use half a bottle for each flower. But the wasps were landing on the flowers one after the other to suck up the accumulated nectar inside. She would have to gauge the timing very carefully.

Silica lurked in a patch of grass ten feet from the first flower and watched the tree at the center of the dome. While it was big, the size of the wasp nest growing on the trunk like a malignant tumor was truly grotesque. Just in her field of view, there were over a hundred wasps going in and out of the nest. Cursors did not appear in this game unless you attacked a target or were targeted in return, so the name of the wasps was still unknown.

According to Friscoll, who'd been scouting the dome before anyone else, the wasps' feeding activity seemed random, but once a wasp had drunk from a flower, no other would visit the same flower for at least thirty seconds. In other words, if you waited until after a wasp had left a flower, you would have a sure-fire chance to insert the lobelia poison.

Up close, the gargamol flowers were quite unpleasant. The bigger ones were a good six feet across. The thick petals were a brilliant reddish-purple with lots of fluorescent green spots. If you stared at it long enough, it was likely to make your eyes flicker.

Real rafflesia flowers had no stalk, growing directly out of the ground, but the gargamol flowers did grow on a trunk about twenty inches long and wide. The honeysucker ticks crawled up the trunk several at a time, sticking their sharp mouths into the tough surface.

A giant wasp lit upon a thick gargamol petal. Its antennae waggled a bit, then it lowered its head toward the vaselike center and stuck it inside. The metallic sheen of the midsection wrinkled as it stretched and contracted. It did not look like any 3D model she'd ever seen.

After ten seconds, the wasp removed its head from the flower, cleaned its mandibles with its forearms, then spread its brown wings and took flight.

Now.

Silica emerged from the grass and ran to the gargamol flower. She pulled out the cork on the bottle of poison and reached as far as she could over the petals. It was just enough to get to the center, so she carefully tilted the bottle.

A blue, barely viscous liquid poured from the mouth of the bottle into the hole in the center of the flower. She eyed about half of the material out and quickly straightened the bottle.

But it was a bit too rough of an action, because a few drops splattered out of the top right past Silica's hand as they fell onto the petals.

She flinched with surprise, then fit the cork firmly back into the mouth of the bottle. Over twenty seconds had passed since the wasp flew away. Ten seconds was the soonest possible time the next wasp might approach.

She crouched and moved away from the gargamol. Once she was back in the patch of grass she wanted, she finally let out the breath she'd been holding.

During the strategy meeting, she assumed that actually applying the poison would be easy, but in practice, it was much trickier. If any of the droplets had landed on her hand earlier, she would have been instantly paralyzed and fallen onto the flower.

Wearing Lisbeth's iron-plated gloves would have given her more poison resistance, but it interfered with the sensation in her fingertips. That was another problem unique to VRMMOs. Silica made a mental note to get some fingerless leather gloves like Kirito wore if anyone she knew had the Leatherworking skill. She ran to the next flower.

The second, third, and fourth poison applications went much smoother, and she was down to her last bottle.

Fifteen minutes had already passed since the mission started— technically, since the lobelia poison was finished. They needed as many wasps as possible to ingest the poison before its effects wore off. There was no time to waste.

She waited impatiently for the wasp to leave the fifth gargamol flower and had just left her hiding spot when she heard a high-pitched screech right behind her.

"Squeeeeee!"

She spun around and saw, about fifteen yards away, a huge dark shape take flight.

At first, she thought it was a mammoth wasp, but quickly realized her mistake. It was *two* wasps, working together to carry something. It was a grassy, fluffy plant. No…

It was a ghillie suit. With Chett inside.

They had her by the head and back, but she was doing nothing, her limbs and tail dangling below her—she had already passed out. Silica looked at her cursor and saw that she still had over 80 percent of her HP, but there was a Debuff icon displaying a poison stinger. One of the wasps must have stung and paralyzed her.

Chett was the smallest and best at hiding of the six of them, so how did she get spotted before anyone else? Whatever the reason, they had to rescue her.

Silica set the bottle on the ground, then stuck her hand into her ghillie suit and squeezed the hilt of the fine steel dagger on her left hip. But the wasps were already twenty feet up in the air. Even a jumping-type sword skill would not help her reach them now.

"...Sinon!" Silica hissed, glancing toward the bridgehead on the south end of the dome.

Sinon was already kneeling at the edge of the structure with her musket at the ready. But a second passed, then another, and the muzzle was not firing.

Shoot! she urged silently, then at last realized what was wrong. The two wasps were overlapping with the paralyzed Chett. Even a crack shot like Sinon would have trouble ensuring a clean, perfect shot of just one of the wasps. But if nothing changed, they were going to take Chett into the nest high overhead.

If only Kirito or Asuna were here! Silica thought.

She clenched her jaw. They were off in the Underworld, doing their best. She couldn't just rely on her knee-jerk reflexes. She had to think for herself now.

Two wasps had spotted and attacked Chett, but none of the others flying around the dome had linked to the action. The wasps probably identified the little Patter as prey, not an enemy. That was why they paralyzed her, rather than killing her on the spot.

It probably meant they wouldn't kill her right away inside the nest. Although it was awful to consider, she probably had some time before the wasps tried to eat her. If they could wipe out the entire colony before then, they could save Chett.

With a great act of will, Silica tore her gaze away from her helpless companion—her friend.

She rushed to pour the lobelia poison into the remaining gargamol flowers, then tossed the empty bottle. She was making her way back toward the bridgehead when she heard something fall to the ground with a thump nearby. It was a paralyzed wasp.

As Chett was a raid member and had been attacked, cursors appeared over the wasp's head. The name there was *Gilnaris Worker Hornet*. The first word was unfamiliar to Silica, but she recognized the last one; hornets were the largest kind of wasps. On the right side of its HP bar was an icon of a blue flower on a black background. The lobelia poison had done the trick and immobilized the wasp with paralyzing venom.

Another one fell…and then another. The wasps were dropping left and right. If they could neutralize half the swarm, then even a midsize raid party of twenty-four—without Chett they were twenty-three—could win this fight.

Above, noticing the change in their fellows, more wasps that hadn't taken any poisoned nectar were buzzing about with alarm. Once the battle was on, the dome was going to devolve into a ferocious battle.

There would be no time to think after that. She'd just have to stay abreast of everything possible and make the best decisions as quickly as she could. The way Kirito and Asuna did, but in her own style.

Silica reached the bridgehead about the same time as Argo, Ceecee, Friscoll, and Dikkos. She pressed her eye to a peephole and saw Chett being taken into the nest.

I'll save you. I guarantee it, Silica swore.

The raid leader, Sinon, called out in fierce tones, "Initiate combat! Construction team, protection team, onward!"

14

The interior of the mystery facility was so quiet, you almost wondered if the guards at the gate were only mannequins.

The downward staircase went on and on. Three, four landings passed, all under weak lighting, and there was still no sign of the next floor. I listened very carefully as we walked, but all I could hear was our footsteps.

Once we had descended a good three floors' worth, I asked a question that had just popped into my head. "Hey, do you think they dug this out with manpower alone...?"

Eolyne gave me a critical sidelong glance. "Do I have to answer that right now?"

"W-well, no, you don't *have* to..."

"Fine, I'll tell you. When performing underground construction on this scale, you'd normally use the dark excavation method."

"D-dark...?"

It took me a few moments to figure out what that meant. Dark elements, when burst, expanded to devour other matter before blinking out of existence. Bedrock deep in the ground would have an incredibly high priority level, so dark elements probably couldn't do anything about that, but the soil would be very low, by contrast. So if you generated a bunch of dark elements on the ground and burst them all, you could dig without needing a shovel or heavy machinery, and you didn't need to worry about all the excess soil, either.

"Ahhh, I get it…but isn't that kind of dangerous? Precise control over dark elements requires a really high mastery of sacred arts, from what I remember."

"That's exactly right. We were only able to safely make use of this method with the light permeation steel plate formula that…"

He paused in the middle of his sentence, then pointed ahead.

After so many landings on the stairs, we had finally come to an end with a single door. At last we'd reached the next floor, but it felt like we'd descended about five floors' worth of space.

Even with the ease of this dark excavation method, it was clearly a major bit of construction. What was it that had to be located so deep underground?

Eolyne and I shared looks of determination, then nodded and snuck down the remaining steps. Even right next to the door, it was utterly silent. I didn't see a keyhole, so I grabbed the pushdown handle and pulled opened the door about two inches.

Through the crack, I could see a hallway of bare metal floor and walls continuing onward. It was dark up close, but lighter farther down.

There were no people where I could see, so I opened the door more and slipped into the corridor. The Night-Sky Blade and Blue Rose Sword plus my full weight together did not cause a single creak in the floor. The iron plates must have been very thick.

Like before, Eolyne took the lead, and I followed. Soon the source of light ahead became clear. A part of the right wall was glass panes, and pale light was shining through from the other side.

There was another door at the end of the corridor, but it had a control panel on it, meaning it was an elevator, not more stairs. So that was the proper means of access, and we'd taken the emergency staircase. The hallway was a straight shot, so if someone came out of the elevator, there was nowhere to hide. Eolyne would have to use that Hollow Incarnation again, but he still looked pale to me. Maybe his weakness to sunlight was just one facet of a general physical weakness.

That was one area where he differed from Eugeo, who looked fragile but was actually extremely tough, I thought, watching the commander walk ahead of me.

We made our way carefully down the hallway, which smelled faintly of iron, until we reached the spot where the wall turned into a glass window. The bottom three feet of the wall was still iron, so we ducked down behind it and carefully lifted our heads to see out.

"......!!"

My eyes were drawn to a stunning sight that almost made me shout out loud.

On the other side of the glass was a shallow, rectangular room; the far wall also had glass windows. Behind it was a space about the size of a gymnasium, and in the center of that was something I found hard to believe.

Black scales, gleaming smoothly. A long, large, coiled body. A pointed tail and a sharply angled wedge-shaped head.

It was a snake. But the size of it was unbelievable. Its body was so thick that even two full-grown adults wouldn't be able to lift it. I couldn't easily guess its length, but it had to be no less than seventy feet long. In length alone, it was probably longer than the dragons the Integrity Knights once rode.

"...A Divine Beast...," Eolyne gasped, his voice trembling with fear and awe.

Divine Beasts. Massive creatures that in the distant past were said to have inhabited various places in the human realm. In game terms, they would be considered "named monsters." But the majority of them were purged by the Integrity Knights on Administrator's orders so they could be turned into the material for powerful weapons, or so I was told. From the ones I'd seen, Eldrie's Frostscale Whip and Deusolbert's Conflagration Bow were both divine weapons derived from these beasts.

"Y-you mean there are Divine Beasts in this age, too?" I asked without thinking.

The young man running the Integrity Pilothood nodded. "Of course there are. But all the Divine Beasts are fiercely protected by Stellar Law, and it's forbidden to even enter their domains. To lock one up underground like this is truly the act of a barbarian who spits in the eye of God..."

The god Eolyne spoke of was probably Stacia, the Goddess of Creation. It felt very strange to think of this in relation to Asuna's beaming face, so all I could summon by way of response was a flat, "Uh-huh."

A number of tubes in colors like red and green ran along the floor of the great chamber, two of which traveled into the great serpent's mouth. The tubes were connected to the body by means of giant, stake-like needles. Most likely, the snake was not simply asleep but kept in a comatose state by some kind of chemical running through the tubes.

I'd killed countless monsters in my time through various virtual worlds, so maybe it wasn't my place to be outraged by this. But all the same, I clenched my fists at the sight.

Eolyne brushed my shoulder then and drew my attention to the snake's head by pointing. "Did you just see something... moving...?"

"Huh...?"

I squinted, staring closely at the snake's great head resting lifelessly on the ground.

Yes, there was definitely something moving in the shadow created by the enormous head. I couldn't make it out clearly because of the two layers of thick glass, but it was squirming and writhing right before the serpent's snout. Could it be...?

"Eo, do you think that's the black snake we were chasing?"

"Oh...I think you're right...but how did it get down here?"

His question was a good one. I pressed my cheek against the glass and looked upward; the ceiling was metal plating just like the walls and floor, and in the corner of the chamber, there was a slatted vent.

"If that's for air circulation, then it must go up to the roof of the structure," I whispered.

Eolyne pressed his face against the glass to see. "Good point. So the place the black snake was born was here...or maybe..."

He didn't finish that sentence, but I knew what he was thinking.

The "thing" that had given birth to the black snake was perhaps the comatose Divine Beast itself. The people managing this facility were causing the Divine Beast to give birth through some means, then implanting parasites into the heads of the babies, feeding dark elements into their bellies, and turning them into biological missiles.

The children of a Divine Beast would surely have high life stats, even as newborns, and it wasn't outlandish for them to have the power of flight, either. You didn't need to go through the effort of raising them, so they were perfect for weapons—but even before the matter of Stellar Law, it was cruel manipulation and utterly inhumane.

The baby snake was trying to wake its mother, poking at the mouth of the great serpent with its tiny snout. But the parent was not budging in the least.

A closer look revealed that on the side of the great snake's head were three eye sockets covered by dark-gray lids. The eyes underneath them would surely be ruby red, just like the baby's. But unless we did something about the chemicals being sent into its mouth, nobody could wake up the serpent.

"Eo...what do we do?"

The pilot commander did not reply at once. After a few seconds, he said with frustration, "It galls me...but there's no way to save the Divine Beast and its child right now. We know the location of the base, so the best course of action would be to return to Cardina, report this to the Stellar Unification Council, and send an official inspection to—"

He broke off. There was a faint metallic sound on the other side of the glass. I turned to look through the window again and saw a thick door on the left wall opening very slowly. Two figures emerged from the side chamber. They seemed very squat, but only because they were wearing suits that completely covered their bodies, like chemical protection suits from the real world.

The two walked right up to the Divine Beast. The suit in the front was carrying a long metal stick in their right hand.

The baby snake was still desperately leaping around its mother's mouth and hadn't noticed them yet. I sent a silent message to *wake up and get away*, but of course it didn't hear me...

The suit in front pointed the metal stick at the juvenile snake. A plier-like tool shot out from the tip and firmly grabbed the little snake's body.

The snake struggled as though it were on fire, but it could not escape the steel pliers. The metal rod retracted to its original length, and the people in protective suits lifted their captured quarry high, talking among themselves.

It was impossible to hear what they were saying thanks to the distance and the glass. I gave Eolyne a look, crouch-walked farther down the hall, opened the door to the room adjacent, and snuck into what seemed to be an observation room for the Divine Beast.

From a speaker box placed high on the wall, I could hear very faint voices talking. Both seemed to be men.

"...*but it can't lay eggs on its own. The last stimulant was eight days ago, so it should be another two weeks before the eggs it's carrying reach the bare minimum size.*"

"*Still, where did this juvenile come from, then? Did we miss it when collecting eggs before, somehow?*"

"*That's hard to imagine, given the steps...but in any case, we've got to deal with this— and fast. Should we prep the juvenile for guided combat again?*"

"*Nah, it's already past the size where we can outfit it. It's too large for the insect to take over its brain entirely. Just gotta dispose of it.*"

Based on the gestures, that statement seemed to be from the man who wasn't holding the metal tool. He opened a case attached to the belt of his suit and pulled out a large syringe.

"*Hold it down tight,*" he said to his partner, and removed the cap from the syringe. Sensing danger, the baby snake struggled even harder, but the arms of the pliers had a firm grip on its neck. There was no escape.

The man lowered the syringe toward it.

The sharp tip approached the snake's throat.

And then, just like that, the needle broke at the base, emitting a high-pitched crack, and a split second later, the rest of the syringe crumbled to pieces, too.

"*Whoa!!*"

"*Wh-what?!*"

The men in protective suits jumped backward in alarm, and Eolyne and I both gasped. We hid under the window, then shared silent looks. It was my Incarnation that shattered the syringe itself, but the needle wasn't my doing, and I couldn't imagine anyone other than the pilot commander could have done that.

Are you sympathizing with it? he had asked me earlier, but I didn't have the chance to point that out now. The little room—and probably the entire base, for that matter—was suddenly full of screaming alarms.

I glanced down into the big room and saw that the men in the protective suits had cast aside the broken syringe and plier rod and were rushing back through the door in the left wall. The liberated baby snake wriggled under the head of the comatose serpent. We'd saved the snake's life, but it was too early to celebrate.

"That was bad…They detected the use of Incarnation," Eolyne whispered.

"Wh-what should we do? Run away?"

"No…It was only an instant that we used it, so they shouldn't have been able to pinpoint our location. It's better to stay hidden in here than rush through the base."

"B-but we're not safe here, eith—"

Before the words were entirely out of my mouth, there was a sound like pressurized air being fired from out in the hallway. I crawled toward the window next to the hallway and peered through. The floor readout on the control panel next to the elevator was moving.

I headed back to my previous spot and said, "The guards are coming."

"Don't worry. I'll use Hollow Incarnation again," Eolyne replied. He grabbed my left arm and pulled me close.

That left my head resting against the commander's right shoulder, which was more than a small surprise, but he had his hand on my back, so I couldn't move anyway.

That strange sensation came over me again. My flesh grew faint and dispersed like mist. Even the feeling of contact with Eolyne's body became indistinct, until I could not tell where I ended and began...

Abruptly, a painful chill shot through my dissipating mind.

In fact, it was not just a simple cold. If anything, it was like dark flame, devouring all heat and light as it swirled...

I heard the door open behind us.

Turning my head just a bit, I tried to catch sight of the source of the chill through my rippling vision.

Black leather boots, polished to a mirror shine, trod upon the steel floor, cutting crisply through the blaring alarms.

15

"Bunker B, durability forty percent!" shouted Holgar, waving his sword.

Next to him and Sinon was a simple shack structure consisting of a ridgepole resting diagonally on two angled pillars, propped up on the sides by logs and tied in place with rope. In outdoorsman terms, it was called an A-frame shelter. The back was open to the air, with no doors or windows or floor, but considering it could be built with a bare minimum of resources, it was surprisingly durable.

However, the open properties window of the shack showed that its durability was down from its maximum of four thousand to less than sixteen hundred. A number of giant wasps stuck to the wall—gilnaris worker hornets, technically—were chewing at the logs with their sharp jaws, delivering constant damage.

"I'll repair it right away. Just hang in there!" shouted Dikkos from off to the right. Holgar shouted back, "Just make it quick!" before swinging his longsword at a wasp that had come diving at him.

The wasp spun and hurtled away thanks to the diagonal slash, but it spread its wings and legs to stabilize itself in midair. At that moment of stillness, Sinon aimed her musket at the base of its six legs and pulled the trigger.

Blam! A dry crack split the air, and the bullet shot through the middle of the creature's chest, a weak point for all insects. The wasp's HP went down to zero, and then it froze in midair before bursting into a million tiny blue particles a few moments later.

"Nice shot!" called out Dikkos, who had just rushed over after repairing Bunker B. He ignored the half dozen wasps clinging to the wall of Bunker A and tapped a log near the entranceway. At the bottom of the window that appeared were four buttons: INFORMATION, TRADE, REPAIR, and DISMANTLE. He promptly hit the REPAIR button, starting a thirty-second countdown.

If Dikkos moved from his current spot or took major damage, the repair would fail, but Holgar deftly held off any wasps that approached. In time, the countdown reached zero. The entire lean-to glowed faintly, and the durability returned to its max value of four thousand.

The ten or so wasps were still stuck to the wall, so the number promptly began dropping again, but they ignored the creatures chewing on the logs. This bunker was both a refuge for people to use while drinking healing potions and a trap to lure the wasps in and keep them distracted, rather than fighting.

Of course, that plan would be ruined if the bunkers were destroyed, but for now, Dikkos and Ceecee were managing to keep the three bunkers repaired. The real question was if the stockpile of logs and ropes for repairs would hold out by the end of the battle.

At last, Sinon finished reloading her musket. She had plenty of bullets, but only a bit over forty uses of blasting powder left. Unfortunately, they didn't seem to be making a dent in the number of wasps.

"All loaded!" she cried, and Holgar gave her a thumbs-up with his sword hand.

Before them were the main attackers: Agil, Klein, and Leafa from *ALO*, Zarion and the insects, and the Bashin warriors, forming a battle line that fought off the descending hornets.

Agil and Klein were as smooth and practiced as ever, and

the rhinoceros beetle Zarion and the stag beetle Beeming had gleaming carapaces that blocked the wasps' venomous stings. On the other hand, the safety of the lightly armored Bashin was a significant concern, but they seemed to have experience fighting giant wasps, because they nimbly avoided the stings and performed powerful counters. It was expert combat, a clear sign that their AI was leagues above the NPC mercenaries you could hire in *GGO*.

Over five minutes had passed since the battle began, and no one on the attacking side had succumbed to paralysis yet. But it was hard to avoid the bites and ramming attacks from above, as the list of HP bars in the upper left showed the front line taking steady, regular damage.

"Tomoshin, pull back and heal!" Sinon shouted. Dikkos's spearman companion waited for the right moment to leave the line, then rushed for Bunker C, the nearest shelter.

In exchange, the cricket Needy rushed out of Bunker B and up to Sinon, black compound eyes gleaming, and said, "I'm in."

"Okay, to the left," Sinon replied in English. Needy rushed off to fill the spot Tomoshin had vacated. Sinon watched the grasshopper go, feeling secretly relieved that she'd been able to communicate properly.

Sinon felt reasonably confident in her English-speaking ability, even if it wasn't quite on the level of Asuna's or Kirito's, but there was a vast difference between getting good scores on tests at school and actually holding a conversation with a native speaker. For a second, she thought, *If I'd just registered for the North American* GGO *server from the start, I might be more fluent by now.* But then she would never have met Kirito in the BoB tournament on the Japan server or become friends with Asuna and the others, and she wouldn't have been here in this battle, fighting giant wasps.

The friend who had invited her to *GGO*, Spiegel—Kyouji Shinkawa—had been taken to a youth medical facility three months ago. Technically, it was more like a juvenile correctional education center for criminally maladjusted youth. While he'd been more of a secondary figure in the Death Gun incident, there had been four homicide victims, so his sentence was going to be very, very long.

Sinon had gone to visit the facility just once, but she hadn't been able to see Kyouji. If only something, some little thing had gone differently, she thought, maybe he wouldn't have gotten involved in that horrible incident. On the other hand, perhaps it had all been inevitable.

At the bare minimum, *Sword Art Online* was at the center of everything. The Death Gun incident, Project Alicization, this *Unital Ring* event, everything tied back to the *SAO* Incident in the end.

Would this really be the final act? Or was this just a step in the process, like everything else?

To know the answer, they'd have to survive and reach the center of the world, the land revealed by the heavenly light. And if Friscoll was right that the continent was designed as a series of raised steps, they couldn't get to the next stage without clearing this wasp lair.

Gotta stay focused.

Sinon swept aside all unnecessary distractions and readied her musket.

Gigantic green wasps continued to fly out of the nest stuck to the giant tree in the center of the dome, but the ten or so frontline fighters were able to hold them off because over half the wasps had been paralyzed by the lobelia poison. There were an almost uncountable number of wasps littering the ground all around, their wings and antennae twitching feebly.

All of that was thanks to Silica, Argo, Chett, and the others for undertaking the dangerous poisoning mission, but now they had to rescue Chett at all costs. Her HP bar was staying at 80 percent, but the wasps could be prepping her to be food for the larvae any moment now.

Once no more fresh wasps were coming out of the nest, they'd hurry and clean up all the paralyzed wasps on the ground, then rescue Chett. But if the wasps on the ground recovered before they had finished off the nest, they'd have no choice but to retreat.

Sinon realized she was clenching her teeth when a friendly voice called out, "Thanks for waiting!"

It was Lisbeth, who had emerged from Bunker A with full health again.

"Go in the middle! Klein, pull back!" Sinon commanded. The katana-user replied, "You got it!" and left the line. A wasp tried to chase him, but Holgar jump-slashed it to keep it back.

Its HP must have been low already, because it split apart before Sinon could even shoot it. Seeing that he was in the clear, Klein started drinking his potion next to the entrance of the bunker, without bothering to go in.

"Hey, Sino-Sino, you think things are going well so far, too?!"

"I warned you, if you call me that again, I'll light you on fire," she threatened, jabbing a finger at Klein. He grinned back at her briefly before eyeing the wasps chewing on the wall of the bunker, checking his own HP bar, and then eyeing the nest twenty yards away. He must've been worried about Chett, too.

The nest had to have a durability rating of its own, so in a pinch, she could destroy it with the Hecate II. But she had only five more 12.7 mm bullets, which she could not replace at the moment, and there was always the possibility she might accidentally hit Chett's location inside the nest.

Plus, the gilnaris worker hornets were tough foes, but there would be many greater obstacles on the way to the center of the world. If you didn't have the strength to tackle those challenges in the intended way, there was no way you'd match the hardy warriors from other worlds like *Asuka Empire* and *Apocalyptic Date*.

We're fine. I know we'll win, Sinon told herself, resuming her orders and shooting.

After several more minutes, her gunpowder stock had fallen under thirty—and the wasps finally stopped flying out of the nest.

"Adds are finished! Wipe out the ones flying now, then the ones stuck to the bunkers, followed by the paralyzed hornets on the ground!" she shouted. The attackers roared back with enthusiasm.

It was nothing short of a marvel that they'd fought for nearly ten minutes and not a single person had taken a poisonous stinger attack. The tell was clear and the attack's range was short, so it wasn't that hard to block with a shield or back-step away, but you couldn't do something like that for so long in a huge, chaotic battle on your first try without very firm willpower.

In that sense, the greatest advantage of Team Kirito was the experience itself of having been through so many events and trials. Of course, there were also many new companions from the past few days, and there would be more in the future. But the main thing was that the bonds holding the team together would only grow stronger with each challenge surpassed.

And that was probably what would be tested in the very end.

Sinon finished reloading her musket and pulled out the ramrod.

But when she lifted her head, what she saw sent a subzero chill through her spine.

The wasp nest, which should have been empty of reinforcements, was active again. Something was appearing from the highest hole of the bunch.

This was the hole big enough to pass the paralyzed Chett through. Now, pushing and cracking its way out was a wasp head with three curved compound eyes, and horrendously menacing jaws. Only this one was at least four or five times larger than the heads of the wasps they'd been defeating thus far.

After the head came a gleaming chest, six legs, and an enormously bulging abdomen. Lastly, a venomous stinger the size of a sword glittered in the flickering sunlight through the leaves.

The gargantuan wasp that came crawling slowly down the side of the nest was easily over six feet long. The green on its head and abdomen was as vivid as an emerald, and its folded wings were orange in tint. Above its head was a cursor with three HP bars. Its title was *Gilnaris Queen Hornet*.

"...There you are, queen bee," Klein said with a grin.

They were fighting an entire nest of wasps, so this should have been a predictable outcome. But even now, through the hole the queen had destroyed on her way out, more wriggling shapes were visible.

Next to appear were wasps smaller than the queen but with notably sharp forms and developed jaws. These were gilnaris soldier hornets, and there were four of them.

The queen and soldier hornets took flight all at once.

Their wings buzzed deeper and louder than the workers, five large shapes in formation. They circled through the air of the dome, gradually spiraling higher and higher.

Sinon quickly glanced around to survey the situation. The flying workers had almost entirely been eliminated. But there were still nearly a hundred paralyzed wasps on the ground from the lobelia poison. Based on their reactions, the paralysis would probably start wearing off in a minute or two. If they were surrounded by this many workers in addition to the queen and soldiers, they wouldn't stand a chance.

It was time to utilize the secret weapon.

Sinon spun around and shouted, "Silica, it's time!"

"Right!"

Two shapes, large and small, burst out of the tunnel at the south end of the dome. The smaller one, of course, was the dagger-user with brown pigtails. The larger one was a quadruped with blackish-brown fur.

Silica and her pet, the thornspike cave bear Misha, had been staying back all through the battle on Sinon's orders, waiting in the safety of the tunnel. If a boss monster happened to show up in the fight, they might need a powerful backup strategy to handle that kind of extra pressure. So Sinon had them in the metaphorical back pocket, but that was the only secret weapon they had. From this point on, it would be an all-out battle in which even the slightest mistake could not be tolerated.

"Silica and Misha, grab the queen's attention and check her temperature! Agil and Klein, Zarion and Beeming, Liz and Leafa, Dikkos and Holgar, work in two-man teams and take one of the guards each! Everyone else, clean up all the workers!" Sinon announced as quickly as she could. The others shouted back to show they were listening.

On the right, with Silica on its back, Misha rumbled forward. His HP recovered, Klein charged after them, determined not to be left out of the fun.

Holgar started up, too, but thought of something and turned back. "Sino-Sino, don't you need a guard while you're loading the gun?"

"I'm fine. I'll use my laser gun if I really need to," she said, patting the Bellatrix SL2 on her left hip.

Holgar smirked and nodded. "All right. Just be careful!" This time, the swordsman continued running after Klein.

When this battle is over, I'm going to need to explain to these men what I mean when I say "no Sino-Sino," Sinon thought. She hoisted the loaded musket and pointed it at the descending queen.

16

Click, click...click.

The polished black leather boots cut across the floor of the little room and stopped in front of the window for observing the captured Divine Beast. Then two more people came through the doorway, halting directly behind the first one. As if on cue, the noisy alarms fell silent.

Eolyne and I were huddled under the window, not ten feet away from the intruders. In my head, I knew we were invisible because of Eolyne's Hollow Incarnation trick, but in practice, I could scarcely breathe.

I didn't even want to move my face, but I couldn't stay staring at the floor the entire time. Careful not to make a sound, I slowly craned my neck upward to catch sight of the intruders—though, really, *we* were the intruders in this base. The side effects of the Incarnate veil over my senses made everything hazy and smoky in outline, but they were close enough that I could just barely make out the finer details.

The two guards in the rear wore the same dark-gray uniform as the ones at the gate up above. But they didn't have the same simple rifles, wearing thin swords on their hips instead. Because of their deep-brimmed hats, their eyes were lost in shadow, but they both seemed to be in their twenties or thirties.

But the person staring into the large chamber in front was difficult for me to identify initially. What was their gender? Were they young or not? I couldn't tell.

They wore a dark-gray coat that extended below the knees. The three-lined sleeve insignia and laced epaulets were a cold silver. They weren't wearing a hat, but between the tall standing collar and richly flowing black hair, the only thing I could see was the sharp, thin bridge of their nose. They seemed a bit taller than me and Eolyne.

The color of their uniforms was not the deep blue of the Integrity Pilots, nor the gray of the Imperial Guard, nor the white of the Central Cathedral security forces.

Earlier, Eolyne mentioned that Admina had its own military command. That might make their uniforms technically the Underworld Space Force's Admina base issue, but if so, it meant that the ones who forced the serpentine Divine Beast to have children in a horrific live experiment and who used guided missiles to damage the X'rphan Mk. 13 were part of Admina's army.

I regretted not asking Eolyne what uniforms the guards at the rear gate were wearing, but it was too late to do anything about it now. The pilot commander was gripping my hand and breathing quickly and shallowly. It wasn't a situation for idle questions like this.

After using Hollow Incarnation to get us through the gate, Eolyne had looked fatigued enough that his face had a blue tint. Now he'd been forced to use it again without an adequate break in between; each and every moment had to be grinding him down. I thought about picking up Eolyne and escaping the little room, but didn't know if we'd be able to disguise the sound of a door opening. All we could do was pray that the trio would leave as soon as possible.

However...

"...The high-intensity Incarnation anomaly was detected by the Incarnameter on this floor, you said?" said the person in the coat, staring down at the larger chamber. Their husky voice was androgynous in sound, so I still couldn't tell their gender.

One of the guards behind them said tensely, "That's right, Your Excellency. The first-floor and rooftop Incarnameters reacted, too, but the highest numbers came from this one in the basement."

The other one added, "Plus, we had a report of unexplained phenomena from our researchers."

"Unexplained?"

"While attempting to administer a solution to the Divine Beast's juvenile in the isolation room, the syringe apparently exploded. The researchers thought the Divine Beast used Incarnation and are refusing to leave the analysis room."

"Hmm..."

The Excellency looked down behind their standing collar, lost in deep thought, until they suddenly pulled their right foot back and turned to face my direction. The movement swung the flowing hair aside to reveal parts of the face that had been hidden.

When I made contact with this person's aura, I thought of powerfully swirling flames of darkness, but their face had a cold, delicate beauty that did not match my initial impression. Their long, narrow eyes were graced with fanciful lashes, and their thin lips were red and bold, their eyes pale blue with streaks of silver.

The moment those icy eyes pointed directly at us, both Eolyne and I tensed. But they soon passed by us, and their attention returned to the hallway window.

"...Are you certain the Avus shot down an enemy dragoncraft?" said the Excellency. The breath of relief I'd been ready to exhale caught in my throat instead.

That confirmed that these were the people who shot the guided missile at the X'rphan. We also learned the name of the large black craft outside, although I didn't know if it meant something.

The real question remaining was whether they realized that they'd attacked the Integrity Pilot commander and member of the Stellar Unification Council, Eolyne Herlentz, himself...

"Yes. The dark-element blast and black smoke were visible to the naked eye. We sent a search party to the area where the craft crashed, just in case, but haven't heard any reports yet saying they've found it," answered one of the guards.

The Excellency faced the large isolation chamber once again. "In that case, it is possible the crew jettisoned before crashing."

"However…even if the riders survived, it would be impossible for them to infiltrate this facility, or even discover it, I feel."

"Hmm…" The Excellency nodded in agreement. They treated this like a teachable lesson for their subordinates. "But Incarnate power is what makes the impossible possible. If you trust your Incarnameter or Incarnate-resistant gear too much, you'll regret it."

"Ah…are you saying someone might have already infiltrated the base, Your Excellency?"

"I wouldn't know about that," said the black-haired beauty, shrugging.

I felt a horrible, spine-freezing chill, and tugged on Eolyne's arm on instinct, pulling us down to the ground as quickly as possible without making noise.

Just after that, the Excellency plunged their right hand inside their coat, removed a saber from their left hip, and drew a line with it in our direction.

We were over six feet away from the saber's range, but I swore I could feel an invisible slash grazing my nose. White sparks jumped from the metal wall just to our right. The impact left a very fine line in the surface as the force continued onward. I was so startled that I didn't deploy an Incarnate wall out of sheer reflex. It was that crisp of a strike.

And the only reason we dodged it was because it was a level swing. If another swing came toward us vertically, there would be no way to avoid it.

Through the heat haze of my vision, I saw the beautiful person pull back their hand and then heard the cool clink of the saber sliding back into its sheath.

"Y-Your Excellency, what is the matter?!" asked the startled guards.

"Nothing at all," the figure said with a wave of their hand. "Sugin, Domhui, return to the ground floor and strengthen defenses at the front and rear entrances. I will investigate the isolation room, just to be sure."

"Then we should join you..."

"No need. Go!" the officer snapped. The two men bolted upright, saluted, and left the little room.

Once they were gone, the Excellency walked to the door on the left wall, which presumably went to the analysis room, as they called it. The door had a grip handle, but the officer stopped before reaching for it.

The Excellency turned back in our direction one more time, and I felt I had to take my eyes off their side profile—it seemed dangerous even to look directly at them. That possibly did the trick, however, because I soon heard the door's heavy sliding as it opened.

More hard footsteps. The door slid again, followed by the click of a latch going into place. Faint footsteps got quieter until they were gone.

Immediately, the haze filtering my vision evaporated. Eolyne had released the Hollow Incarnation. I patted his back; his full weight was resting on me.

"Good job. You saved us," I whispered, relieved. "Now, let's get out of this base while we have the—"

I stopped short. Eolyne slid off me and onto the floor.

17

The first action the gilnaris queen hornet took was not a charge attack, as Silica expected, nor a bite, nor even a poison stinger.

Hovering about five yards off the ground, the queen opened scissorlike jaws and emitted an unearthly screech.

It was a supremely unpleasant frequency, like a cacophony of abrasive metal objects scraping together. It was hard to believe the sound filling Silica's eardrums could be a virtual signal sent by the AmuSphere into her brain, and she couldn't help but cover her ears with her hands. On her shoulder, Pina wailed pitifully. It was an attack directly on the senses, not a kind of system-based status effect, but she had never experienced something so powerful before.

On her left and right, others were hunched over the same way. Silica was about as experienced a VRMMO player as there could be, and this was new to her, so it had to have taken others like Holgar by complete surprise. Even the insects, which did not have visible ears, were covering the sides of their heads. It would have seemed funny…if it were possible to think about anything in this situation.

Bzzz! The four soldier hornets charged. It was a simple body-blow attack, but when a human-sized creature covered in tough armor came hurtling toward you at high speed, the force was greater than a critical hit from a two-handed hammer.

"Gwah!"

"Aieee!"

Deep bellows and high-pitched screams ensued as the eight attackers aside from Silica and Misha were knocked off their feet.

On the left side of her view, eight HP bars lost a big chunk. The biggest damage happened to Leafa, who was high-level but put all her points into attack and wore light armor.

"Leafa!" Silica cried, starting to rush her way. But Leafa, despite a stun effect visible over her head, bravely shouted back, "I...I'm fine! Focus on your role!"

"......!"

Silica grit her teeth and faced forward. The queen wasp was already recovering from the delay after the sonic attack. The next attack would be coming in a second or two. If it was poison or an area-based physical attack, it might actually break down the front line.

Her job was to draw the queen's aggro—more precisely, to have Misha draw it. But as long as the queen was hovering twenty feet in the air, even Misha couldn't reach far enough to hit it with teeth or claws.

There was only one option remaining. It was a major attack that couldn't be repeated, but it'd be the height of foolishness to put yourself in a corner because you didn't want to use up your secret weapon.

"Misha, Thornspike!"

On her command, Misha reared back on its hind legs and spread its front paws wide.

The queen curled up in midair, fearsomely long stinger shining red.

Silica had a sudden intuition that a poisonous area attack was coming. But the attack was just a split second too late.

"Groaaaah!"

The lightning pattern in the fur on Misha's chest glowed as

silver lights shot out of it. It was the namesake of the thornspike cave bear, a special attack that transformed fur into steel quills that shot at the enemy.

The storm of needles, which had wiped out Schulz's team and nearly shot down Mutasina, struck the queen and the four soldiers at her sides directly.

"Greeeee!"

The five hornets screamed in a hideously metallic way and flew over ten yards backward with the force of the attack. The queen took the brunt of the damage, losing nearly 80 percent of her first HP bar. Her guards lost half their health, too.

"Can you manage, Silica?!" Sinon asked from the rear. Silica held up her hand and replied, "I'm all right!"

"Got it! Argo, continue cleaning up!" Sinon called out. From the back of the dome came an energetic "No sweat!" Argo, Friscoll, Needy, the Bashin, and the Patter were finishing off the paralyzed hornets in quick fashion. It took only one or two blows to the neck or chest, where they were most vulnerable, but there were just so *many* of them. It would take at least five minutes before any of the cleanup crew could join the fight against the boss.

"Great job, Silica!" said Agil.

"What a relief!" followed Zarion in English. They had just recovered from the stunning effect of the body blows. The stun icons on the other frontline party members' HP bars were blinking, too.

But the queen and her soldiers were stable again after taking Misha's big attack, also, and were closing the distance once more.

Most likely, their basic tactical pattern was for the soldiers to repeat physical attacks while the queen performed a number of special attacks from a high altitude out of weapon range. If they finished off the soldiers, the queen might fly lower, but the group would certainly take more than one area attack in the meantime.

For now, it was only Sinon's musket that could hit the queen. If Silica told her she couldn't withstand the queen's attack pressure,

Sinon would help, but as the leader of twenty-three, her main duty was to give orders.

Silica and Misha were waiting back in the tunnel for when the boss showed up. There was no way they could use their special attack once and call it a day.

She glared at the descending queen and thought hard. *What would Kirito do here?*

After the *UR* incident began, Kirito continued to break through difficult situations with his trademark outside-the-box thinking and proactive style. Dumping loads of logs from the roof to crush monsters, using temporary construction ghost objects as a visual impediment, firing his ghastly Rotten Shot inside his own mouth to break out of the feeling of suffocation—Silica didn't have that kind of ingenuity, but there had to be something she could try that would help.

She was at least ten feet too short to hit the queen hornet with a weapon. Lisbeth could use the Carpentry skill to build a scaffold, but monster AI in *Unital Ring* were sophisticated, and the queen would probably just move out of range again. Maybe a movable scaffold would work, but there wasn't going to be anything like that in the construction menu...

And that was when an idea took form. It was so perfectly simple that Silica was momentarily dumbfounded. She had to shake off her hesitation and act.

She placed a hand on Misha's side—the bear was glaring up at the queen overhead—and jumped as high as she could, climbing the beast's furry back so she could get on its shoulders.

"Misha, stand!"

"*Grau!*" the bear growled and straightened. Its shoulders rose, lifting Silica like an elevator. Naturally, the angle of her feet changed, too, but she'd be a poor excuse for a light, nimble fighter if she couldn't handle that.

Misha was larger than a real-life brown bear, and when it stood on its hind legs, its shoulders were over ten feet above the ground. Silica had the second-smallest avatar of anyone after Yui, but if she used a sword skill from this position, she should be able to reach the queen at fifteen feet high.

The wasp seemed to recognize this, too, and stopped to hover. But the four guards were approaching slowly from a low height. Apparently, the needle attack had transferred their aggro to Misha. However...

"You're supposed to be fighting *us!*" bellowed Klein, who came running up to do a tremendous jump slash. He was using a scimitar rather than a Japanese-style katana, but Lisbeth had forged the weapon to be as long as possible on his request, and it was enough to just barely reach the soldier hornet's belly.

Following him, Leafa, Dikkos, and Holgar leaped as well, slashing at the remaining soldiers. The hornets' attention turned to them, and the four resumed buzzing angrily around the players.

In the back, the queen opened her jaws as far as she could again: the setup for the sonic attack.

"Forward, Misha!" she instructed. The bear stomped toward the queen. Silica waited for the right moment, then activated her sword skill in the air: the single thrust Rapid Bite.

Silica's inherited skill from *ALO* was Short Swords, but since her proficiency fell down to 100, she couldn't use the high-ranking four- and five-part skills for now. Still, a single-hit skill should be enough to sabotage a special attack activation—*should.*

Stop! she willed, slamming the tip of the dagger into the queen hornet's mouth.

At present, they'd only been able to mine iron ore, so they wouldn't be able to make steel weapons for a while. Silica's fine steel dagger was made with steel ingots gained from melting Kirito's favorite sword from *ALO*, Blárkveld. In other words, this dagger had originally been Kirito's sword.

Of course, the source of the resources wouldn't make a difference on the specs of the result, but in a tense battle that could go either way, your *feelings* might be enough to affect the outcome of the fight. With her righteous weapon in hand, Silica pierced the queen's defense with a fierce blow and not only stopped the sonic attack before it could start but also knocked back the creature, which was twice her size.

"*Gyashhh!*" the enemy hissed with fury. Silica did a backflip in midair and landed on Misha's shoulders. Pina came back down to land on Silica's head, too, and squeaked "*Pyui!*" with pride.

"Nice one, Silica!" cheered Lisbeth from the ground.

"Only thanks to the dagger you made for me, Liz!" she shouted back. *And thanks to Kirito's ingots.*

As for the queen, Silica's Rapid Bite had been a critical hit, and the boss's first HP bar was now gone. There were two left, but this probably meant a change in attack patterns. She would have to keep handling the queen safely and ensuring that every attempt at an area attack was prevented.

The queen had recovered from the knockback and came rushing forward again. Her matte-finish compound eyes had no eyelids or pupils, but somehow, they expressed anger anyway.

"*Gyiii!*" the queen snarled threateningly. Silica stared boldly right back at it.

All around them were the sounds of furious battle between the four soldier hornets and the eight players fighting them. As long as she could keep the queen off-balance and occupied until the soldiers were wiped out, victory was assured.

Just hang in there, Chett. We'll rescue you soon, she told the distant nest, squeezing her dagger.

At that moment, the queen's cutting-machine jaws opened slightly, the sharp mouth behind it twisting. Almost like a mocking smile.

The queen hornet rose higher. Six yards, seven…At this point, Silica couldn't reach her even using Misha's shoulders for a lift.

Did the queen have a hidden attack that could hit the ground from that height? If that was the boss's special, most dangerous trick, she had to stop it somehow. Throw the dagger? No. A Throwing Weapons sword skill might be one thing, but simply hurling an item wasn't going to cancel out a major attack.

Hovering at over twenty-five feet, the queen confirmed Silica's fears by starting a motion she hadn't used before.

The giant wasp's body curled up as round as it could go, compressing the legs. Its long antennae stood erect, and pale light shone from the ends, then started traveling up the antennae. If the lights reached the base, something very bad would happen.

"Sinon!" Silica shrieked, fighting back against a chill that threatened to engulf her whole body. "Shoot it!"

The raid leader must have sensed the danger already. At almost the exact moment Silica cried out, there was the dry crack of a musket.

The queen's left antenna broke off right along the middle.

It spoke to Sinon's shooting skill that she could hit a narrow antenna with a gun as clumsy as a musket. But it was a fraction of a second too late. The light passed through the point where it split just before it happened and reached the queen's head after all.

The triangular array of eyes flashed so brightly you couldn't look directly at it. The light turned into a ring that spread to cover the entire dome.

That was all. There was no damage to Silica, Misha, or any of their companions, and there was no TP or SP loss. No Debuffs, either, it seemed.

Then what did the attack do…? Silica was at a loss.

A low hum began to fill the dome. It rose in volume very quickly: the buzzing of wings. The worker wasps that had been paralyzed by the lobelia poison were getting up off the ground.

The blue light wasn't an attack meant for the players. It was a special technique that removed all Debuffs from the other hornets.

"Cleanup team, gather around Misha!" Sinon commanded. The scattered players all around the dome began racing back. Workers rose and began to congregate as well. There were at least forty—no, fifty of them.

The queen and soldiers were dangerous enough enemies as it

was, but if they got surrounded by this many workers on top of that, even retreating might be difficult. Silica was utterly stunned by this development.

Overhead, the gilnaris queen hornet's mouth once again curved into a mocking smile.

18

"Eo…! You all right, Eolyne?!" I hissed as quietly as I could.

His body, dressed in the dark-blue uniform of the Integrity Pilots, lay slack on the ground, and behind the mask, his eyes were closed. I put a finger to his neck; unlike in regular VRMMOs, you *could* detect a pulse here, but his was very weak, and his skin was shockingly cold.

I had a feeling it was an effect of using Hollow Incarnation twice in quick succession like this, but I had no idea how to help him recover. I'd given him a healing solution after the first time, but it hadn't had any apparent effect beyond helping freshen him up a bit.

He needed rest in a safe location. That was the only way, I decided. I sat up, put my arms around his torso, and lifted.

Suddenly, a piercing pang of sorrow stole my breath. It took me a moment to understand why.

This was so similar to the top floor of Central Cathedral, just after defeating Administrator. So similar to when I had lifted Eugeo, who had been fatally wounded.

The grief and longing that had crystallized in my heart began to loosen and melt, running through my veins again. The sound of my late friend's voice came faintly to my ears:

Our paths separate here...but our memories remain eternal.
And it means we'll be friends forever.

Then he gave name to the sword that still hung on my hip before leaving the Underworld forever. His lightcube reinitialized, and his fluctlight was gone.

Was I still searching for Eugeo's shadow within Eolyne, despite knowing all this? I had thought that when I saw Eolyne's unit ID in the mechamobile, too, but realizing it was completely different from Eugeo's, I had sworn to stop chasing impossible miracles.

I shut my eyes and tried to stop the thoughts.

At this moment, the only thing I should be thinking about was getting Eolyne out of here.

The Excellency had ordered security to be strengthened around the first-floor exits. I couldn't use Hollow Incarnation, so there was no way to get past them without being spotted. If I wanted to give up on stealth, I could just burst through all the floors of the building to the roof, but whoever was making use of this base would go into hiding and possibly kill the Divine Beast to hide the evidence of their actions.

So no—I had to escape quietly.

With that in mind, I lifted up a few more inches and peered into the isolation chamber through the window. The door to the analysis room on the left wall had just opened, and the authority figure and two researchers were emerging.

The researchers were still wearing their protective suits, but the Excellency wore only the coat. Despite being over sixty feet away, the figure's freezing aura and unearthly beauty were palpable from here.

The trio came to a stop some distance away from the comatose black serpent. The Excellency then approached, close enough to touch the beast, and peered right into the massive mouth with the tubes running inside.

"...*The stasis measures seem to be holding up as desired*," the person said, voice audible through the speaker in the ceiling.

One of the researchers replied, "*Th-that is true... The chemicals are being administered in the proper dosages.*"

"*Good. And where is the juvenile you say you've found?*"

"*W-well...*"

The researchers looked at each other, both seemingly resisting the pressure to report first. Eventually, one of them gave up and said, "*We...we lost sight of it when we evacuated the chamber. I believe it should still be somewhere in here...*"

"*In other words, both the juvenile's source and destination are unknown.*"

"*W-well...at present, I suppose that is true...*"

"*Find it and capture it.*"

Their voice was so cold that even separated by thick glass and so much space, I hunched my shoulders guiltily. The researchers shot upright in terror, but did muster up a brave attempt at a rebuttal.

"*B-but, Master Istar...if we attack a juvenile, we might once again draw an Incarnate attack from the Divine Beast...*"

That told me the researchers believed that when Eolyne and I destroyed the syringe with Incarnation, it was the work of the Divine Beast itself.

No, wait a second. Didn't they just say a name? Is...Istar. That's what it sounded like to me. I don't know if that's the first name or last name, but that is the name of our Excellency down there. It sounds like the Mesopotamian goddess Ishtar, but I doubt there's a connection...

Istar turned on their heel, coat swaying, and faced the researchers directly.

Under the bright lights of the isolation chamber, I could see that their flowing black hair actually had reddish highlights. Between that and the pale-blue eyes, my initial impression of cold flame seemed quite accurate still. I would never want to be in the path of that gaze if I were one of those subordinates.

"*...Even if the Incarnate attack came from the Divine Beast, the* *target was the syringe, wasn't it?"* said Istar, cold voice now containing a hint of irritation.

The researchers stood at attention again. *"Y-yes...that is...accurate, but..."*

"In other words, if you do not attempt to kill the juvenile, you will be safe. If you wish to continue this argument, I would be happy to do so in the interrogation room above."

"N-no, Your Excellency! We have no quarrel! We'll begin searching for the juvenile now!"

The researchers were apparently soldiers, too, because they saluted through their protective helmets and then split up to search. It wasn't much of one, because there were absolutely no machines or containers or anything of the like in the isolation chamber, only tubes on the floor coming from the wall to the left, and the coiled Divine Beast in the center. The "juvenile," the baby snake Eolyne and I had followed here, could only hide behind the tubes or under the beast. As a matter of fact, when we destroyed the syringe, I saw it wriggle under the Divine Beast's head.

The two researchers lifted smaller tubes and peered behind larger ones for now, but they would eventually try under the creature. While it was a juvenile, the baby was three feet long and nearly two inches thick, so once the light hit it, there was no way for it to hide and go unnoticed.

Istar watched the researchers work, arms folded. If we were going to escape to the first floor, now was probably the time. Besides, if Eolyne hadn't trapped the baby snake in frost elements and I hadn't healed it with dark elements, it would have blown up and died already.

"......"

My eyes fell on Eolyne, who was still unconscious in my arms.

When the researchers tried to poison and kill the juvenile, I was the one who had destroyed the syringe bottle with Incarnation, but it was Eolyne who shattered the needle itself. In other words, despite his air of calm rationality, the pilot commander possessed enough emotion to perform a risky maneuver to rescue a strange, alien creature. I didn't want to completely disregard and betray that emotion.

Wasn't there some way we could escape from this base *with* the baby snake?

Say, covering our faces with cloth, then breaking the glass window right here, scooping up the little creature, racing up the stairs, and trying to force our way out the back door...?

I might be able to pull off something like that alone, but the slash Istar produced was so fast it rivaled the speed of the onetime elite Integrity Knights. If I had to go into battle with an unconscious Eolyne under my arm, there was no guarantee I would make it out unharmed. Plus, if they learned we had infiltrated them, they might tear down the base before an investigation team could arrive from Cardina anyway. In the end, whether or not I used Incarnation, it seemed that sheer force could not solve the problem...

But wait. Hold on.

Couldn't I use as much Incarnation as I wanted right now, and they wouldn't know it was me? For one thing, their Incarnameters only raised a fuss in response to the strength of the Incarnation and couldn't even point in the direction of the signal source. Of course, I couldn't jump out into the open and raise hell, but if I used Incarnation in some way that convinced them it was the Divine Beast...

I stared up at the ceiling of the isolation chamber. It was dark in the middle, where the light didn't reach, but I could make out what looked like a large square hatch. It had to be a transport route up to the roof, which they'd used to bring the Divine Beast inside.

On the floor, the enormous snake lay limp. I said a silent apology for using it as a replacement or a hiding spot, picked up Eolyne under the arms, exhaled, inhaled...

"......!!"

I unleashed my imagination in a way that was more significant than before, at least one or two gears higher.

The Divine Beast's many eyes glowed red. Its massive head rose quickly. The catheter tubes stuck in its mouth and body pulled out easily, spilling toxic-colored chemicals as they came loose. A moment later, the sirens attached to the Incarnameters began blaring again.

"Aaaah!!"

"Wh-what happened?!"

The researchers inspecting the tubes fell on their bottoms. But Istar merely took a step back, watching the Divine Beast without drawing that sword. It was important they didn't have time to see through my ruse.

The hatch on the ceiling wrenched downward in a shower of sparks. As I suspected, it was nothing but a dark hole on the other side. One of the two thick hatch panels landed near one of the researchers, and the other fell right before Istar, creating even more sparks and a tremendous noise. Even Istar had to jump out of the way of that one.

At the same exact moment, a small and thin—only in comparison to the giant serpent—shape lifted off the floor and attached to the Divine Beast's head, although the three humans would not have seen it.

This would be the climax of a great, dramatic escape.

The Divine Beast's eyes flashed again.

The metal walls of the isolation chamber and the glass window before my eyes shattered to pieces, shooting many glittering pieces through the air.

Soon after, all of it was converted to dark elements. There was absolutely not enough spatial resource to directly generate this many dark elements all at once, but by converting matter, you could make as much as you wanted, so shattering the window was killing two birds with one stone.

The multitude of elements immediately formed a mist configuration, clouding the isolation chamber with purple gloom. I hugged Eolyne to my side, placed my foot on the window frame, and leaped for all I was worth.

I used no wind elements, jumping with nothing but pure Incarnation. We passed through absolute darkness and up into the ceiling hatch. I didn't forget the Divine Beast, either, pulling it along with Incarnate Arms.

Soon the mist of darkness thinned out, and a red light was visible ahead. It was after three o'clock on Centoria right now, which meant it would just be dawn on Admina.

I flew up the square transport tunnel at full speed until I burst through into the sunrise. For an instant I glanced down, just long enough to register the many guards rushing out of the front and rear entrances of the base. Only a minute or two had passed since the incident in the isolation chamber underground; their reaction speed was tremendous. If I wasn't quick about it, they'd spot us.

Focus on the sky. I shot upward, pulling the Divine Beast behind me. We shot through dense-looking clouds and out the other side, putting us above the clouds in just seconds. They wouldn't be able to see us from the ground now.

At last, I could let out the breath I'd been holding. The first thing to do was check on Eolyne. He was still unconscious, but it did seem as though his cheeks were slightly more colored than before. Another bit of relief, then.

To the left, the black serpent floated, using the white clouds as a bed. Its six eyes were covered with gray membranes. The red lights underground were a bit of sleight of hand, using the light from heat elements with steel-element mirrors to make it appear as though the eyes were open and baleful.

All the tubes that had been administering chemicals were gone, but whatever "stasis measures" Istar mentioned being applied would probably take longer to wear off. Plus, there was no guarantee the beast would be friendly to us if it woke up. To a Divine Beast, we were just as human as Istar, so it was probably more likely to simply attack with no provocation.

So the best thing to do was to return the Divine Beast to its domain before it woke up. But then it might just get captured by the people at the base again.

What to do? I had to come up with an answer.

Just then, I heard a discordant *gweee!* right behind me and felt a burning, piercing pain shoot from my back through my chest.

19

After it was all over and she had time to think again, Silica realized that, despite the danger they'd been in, she'd never once lamented the lack of Kirito, Asuna, and Alice.

The only things she'd thought about were how to get through the situation with the people and weapons they had at the moment.

The worker wasps pressing in from all directions weren't that impressive in terms of stats, but the long-term paralysis their poison caused from just a single sting was extremely dangerous. They'd focused hard on preventing anyone from being surrounded by multiple wasps because avoiding that poison attack was the absolute top priority.

But once the queen and soldiers had a fresh swarm of workers at their side, they suddenly outnumbered the human group two to one. That meant people were going to get targeted by two or more wasps at the same time; even a veteran player would have difficulty if attacked from opposite directions at once. If multiple people got paralyzed and the formation broke down, it might even be difficult to retreat outside the dome.

Sinon's brain must have been burning itself out wondering whether to give the withdrawal order.

There were just ten seconds until the cleanup team with Argo and Friscoll could regroup with the frontline team. In another ten seconds, the workers would be surrounding everyone. Sinon had to do some very tricky calculations before that point. If they retreated now, the hopes of saving Chett from the nest would be snuffed out.

It was just an NPC from just a game, as nearly every player in *Unital Ring* would think. But Silica had come into contact with many NPCs, many AIs, through *SAO*, *ALO*, and the Underworld, and she couldn't classify them as "just" programs anymore. She knew the others would feel the same way, and even their new friends from this world like Zarion and Holgar would probably agree now. They'd sat around the fire with the Bashin and Patter in Ruis na Ríg and shared drinks with them, after all.

I want to save Chett.

As if to mock that very wish just as she made it, the HP bar for Chett on the left edge of her vision dropped slightly but surely.

There was no way to know what was happening inside the nest. But their leeway on the rescue was now over, and Chett was taking damage. Based on the rate of the decrease, it would reach zero in less than a minute.

If there was any hope to overturn this devastating development, it was simple: Kill the gilnaris queen hornet controlling all the hornets.

But the queen still had two whole HP bars, and more importantly, at a height of over twenty-five feet off the ground, there was no way to hit her. Misha's thornspike attack was on cooldown, and even Agil's ax wouldn't be anywhere near long enough to hit if he stood on the bear's shoulders instead.

If only we could drag the queen down to the ground—!

Silica gritted her teeth so hard they could have cracked. All seemed lost.

"Silica!" shouted a voice with a particularly fluid enunciation. In high-speed English, the voice continued, "Move and have Misha squat down!"

Either her practical English lessons at the returnee school

helped her pick out the words or some kind of frantic emergency telepathy was doing the trick. Silica immediately hopped off of Misha's shoulders and commanded, "Misha, get down!"

The bear reacted instantly, its front paws landing heavily on the ground. Behind it, a shadow leaped speedily into the air. Its form was flowing and had extremely lengthy legs: the grasshopper Needy.

He raced up to Misha's shoulder, squatted briefly, then shot upward in a huge leap like he'd been shot from a cannon.

It was the kind of jump that only a grasshopper could make, not the other *Insectsite* players and certainly not any of the humans. The brown body soared toward the queen hornet high overhead. Although using Misha as a trampoline added seven feet to the floor, he still jumped well over fifteen feet just on his own.

Needy's arms closed in on the queen's rear legs. He was planning to grab her and weigh her down.

But the queen's wings buzzed, anticipating this attempt, and she rose even higher.

Needy's hands swung and hit only air—

Or so it seemed.

At the last second, the grasshopper opened his mouth and shot white thread upward. It was the special cricket web he'd shot to capture Friscoll when the man was a scout for Mutasina.

The thread wrapped around the queen's long stinger, and Needy's descent after the apex of his jump was halted with a hefty jerk. The added weight caused the queen's ascent to stop, too. But she wasn't falling, either. Her climbing ability and Needy's weight were canceling each other out.

A number of yellowish-green lines of light crossed the space over Silica's head. Sinon was firing her special laser gun rather than the musket. She was aiming for the queen's wings rather than its body. The superheated bolts were punching burning holes in the delicate membranes of the insect wings.

At last, the queen hornet began to drop.

This is it. Our final chance.

The moment the queen hit the ground, they'd deliver a concentrated group attack on her weak points. But over half the group's damage dealers were fighting the soldier hornets, and in *Unital Ring*, where stray attacks could hurt your fellow players, there was a limit of only five or six players who could safely hit the queen at the same time. Even if all six of them used their best sword skills, that wasn't likely to eliminate both remaining HP bars.

There has to be something that can do more damage than sword skills. Something, something...

Silica felt her brain burning, racing into overdrive as the queen slowly descended, Needy dangling from her stinger.

And then things she'd witnessed before flashed across her mind in quick succession: logs tumbling off the roof of the log cabin. The Hecate II propped up on sturdy supports. Two images that fused into a single idea.

"Everybody, surround the spot where she falls!" she yelled, then realized that saying "everybody" might summon more people than the ones she actually wanted. Thankfully, those few—Lisbeth, Klein, Agil, and Leafa—were the very ones who reacted quickest.

They left Zarion, Beeming, Holgar, and Dikkos behind to handle the soldiers, and rushed to the spot where the queen was going to fall, as Silica instructed.

"Hold your weapon aloft with your left hand and open your equipment menu with your right!"

All of them were right-handed. If they practiced executing a sword skill with their left hand, the precision would always be poorer than if right-handed. But the four of them did exactly as she said, switching their weapons to their nondominant hands and raising them. Then they rotated their right hands to bring up the ring menu.

Silica's dagger, Lisbeth's mace, Klein's scimitar, Agil's two-handed ax, and Leafa's longsword made a circle, in the center of which landed Needy.

He grabbed the thread coming from his mouth with both hands and yanked the queen with it, then leaped away, out of the circle.

A moment later, the queen's seven-foot-plus body crashed into the ground. A faint stun effect appeared over the hornet's head, but that would not last long.

The final order:

"Change the weapon in your left hand to your inherited weapon!"

They must have realized what she was asking for by now. The words hadn't even fully left her mouth when the four of them rotated their equipment wheel and hit the selection button.

Five raised weapons made of iron flashed white and vanished, replaced by dazzling weapons of the highest quality:

Silica's dagger, Issreidr.

Leafa's longsword, Lysavindr.

Agil's ax, Notthjorr.

Klein's sword, Spirit Katana Kagutsuchi.

And Lisbeth's hammer, Lightning Hammer Mjölnir.

These weapons, brought over from *ALO*, required more strength than anyone possessed, like Sinon's Hecate II, and even approaching level-20, no one could even lift them.

But if summoned to a hand held overhead, there was nothing stopping you from dropping it straight down. Controlling their fall by the inch might be hard, but the queen hornet's weakness, her midsection, was still about as big as a midsize car tire.

"*Ryaaaah!*" Silica roared, uncharacteristically ferocious, giving everything she had to adjust a dagger as heavy as a boulder as it fell and slamming it onto the base of the queen's leg as it lay on its back.

Her companions' inherited weapons all did the same, creating a thunderous roar all around, severing the thick carapace in a tightly formed circle.

20

The first worry that ran through my head was that whatever pierced my body might have hit Eolyne.

But it seemed it only grazed his bangs where I was holding him to my side and continued on through nothingness. I almost felt relief at that, but couldn't allow myself to relax. I deployed an Incarnate shield and quickly turned around.

At the edge of my cotton-white cloud was a figure so dark they were like a blot of spilled ink.

A person, dressed in black, long hair and coat hem flapping in the wind, just floating there. Their right hand, extended toward me, was holding what looked like a large gun. It was a bullet that had gone through my breast.

I've been shot, I thought, and immediately felt the burning pain return. I looked down to see a hole big enough to fit a finger inside, just below my collarbone, out of which blood was spurting.

While it hadn't hit my heart directly, I would previously have lost half my life value and then bled out the other half over time. But after my battles with Administrator and Gabriel Miller as the God of Darkness, Vecta, I learned that my flesh in this world was nothing more than a projection of my soul.

Thinking back on the time when Gabriel had blown away my

lower half and carved out my heart, this barely even qualified as a wound. I used the resource of my own blood to heal the bullet wound and repaired the uniform while I was at it.

If I could have used even half this level of Incarnation in the fight against Administrator, maybe I could have saved Eugeo, I thought, a brief moment of longing regret. I stared down the distant silhouette.

The rising sun was behind the figure, who was nearly a hundred yards away, so I couldn't see their face, but I could tell from the person's bearing alone that it was the Excellency we saw in the base: Istar. It was alarming that Istar had immediately tracked us in the midst of all that chaos, but more important was the question of *how* they were flying.

Should I approach to glean more information, or prioritize the safety of Eolyne and the Divine Beast and flee, or just launch into a preemptive attack?

The figure took advantage of my indecision and moved. Long coat whipping like black wings, they closed the gap with unbelievable speed. On pure reaction, I expanded my Incarnate wall and strengthened its output, too.

I expected that at their current speed, the figure would slam into the invisible wall hard enough that they would break every bone in their body. Instead, they came to a stop so suddenly that they could have left skid marks in the air, just inches away from my defensive wall.

We were no more than thirty feet apart. Below wavy black hair, icy blue eyes cast a steely spell.

Staring into Istar's face head-on, I was once again struck by their inhuman beauty. I hadn't felt awe toward a simple personal appearance since facing off against Administrator.

Istar's face was utterly placid, without emotion, and they said nothing for a good five seconds, examining me and then the unconscious Eolyne. At last, I felt as though I saw the faintest hint of something cross the space between their brows, but then it was gone just as fast.

The figure gazed into my eyes again and finally opened crimson lips. "I apologize for shooting you from behind without warning. I wanted to test it first to see if it would work."

Istar raised the gun and tilted it to demonstrate their meaning. Hearing such an insincere response finally gave me the presence of mind to think, *Oh, you asshole.* Without taking down the Incarnate shield, I threw a verbal jab of my own.

"Did you shoot me there on purpose? Or did you just miss my head or my heart?"

"It's not realistic to aim for any particular spot at that distance. It was a major success just to hit you anywhere at all."

It was the equivalent of a careless shrug, but this was a shot of nearly a hundred yards that hit me on the first try. I recalled Sinon saying that the effective firing range of a handgun in the real world was maybe twenty yards at best, and fifty in *GGO*. Istar's gun was a crude-looking thing, clearly a prototype, and it didn't seem like a high-performance gun. After the lightning-speed slash in the observation room, Istar was an ace sniper, too?

"...How is that gun firing bullets?" I asked, recalling the strange sound it had made. I didn't expect an answer, but Istar looked at the gun and gave me one.

"It's a simple mechanism, just expelling the bullet with the release pressure of a wind element. Though there's a trick in the regulating mechanism to let off excess pressure in the compression chamber."

"I see..."

So that ugly noise was probably from this "regulating mechanism," then. I was still curious as to how it worked, but it seemed like asking to see it would be awkward.

Perhaps even more remarkable was that we were having a conversation at this closer distance, yet I still couldn't be sure if Istar was male or female. Their husky voice, their unearthly beauty, and even their height, build, and uniform were perfectly androgynous, preventing even an educated guess.

At the very minimum, however, I didn't see any little propellers or jet engines, so it was unquestionable that they were flying with Incarnation alone, just like me.

In a sense, Incarnation was the power to overturn the rules of the world with your own imagination, so despite the simplicity of flight itself, the strength of the Incarnation required was astounding. After all, the common knowledge that "people can't fly" existed in the heads of every Underworlder, including the wielder.

As far as I knew, only Administrator and Vecta were capable of absolute Incarnation flight, and if not for the battles we had, I certainly wouldn't have reached my current state, either.

Meaning Istar had either experienced battle on that scale or somehow achieved Administrator-level willpower independently, I thought, staring into those icy blue eyes.

"I have answered two of your questions, so you ought to answer the same number," said Istar, returning the large pistol to a holster on their right side.

Hang on—you owed me because you shot me! I protested silently. But I knew if I wanted to extract information, prolonging the conversation was the way to do it, and Eolyne would eventually recover, too. I was a bit worried about what the Divine Beast floating behind me might do if it awoke, but I could always surround it with a shell of Incarnation and figure it out from there.

"...Sure, if it's something I *can* answer," I replied.

Istar's question was immediate and unexpected. "Were you the one who eliminated the Abyssal Horror?"

For an instant, I wasn't sure if I should answer. If I said yes, I might be giving a benchmark with which to measure my Incarnation level. But I doubted it would end the conversation and cause Istar to attack me.

"That's right."

I didn't mention that it wasn't just me. If that made me seem more powerful than I really was, all the better.

"I see..."

Istar appeared to consider this information, long hair whipping in the cold wind.

Far in the distance, the red sun was slowly but surely continuing its ascent. In the real world, it would be four o'clock soon. At five, I would be pulled out by Dr. Koujiro, along with Asuna and Alice. My chances of getting back to Central Cathedral by then were totally devastated—the X'rphan needed to be repaired before it could fly—but I at least needed to get to a situation where I could afford to simply disappear without warning.

If I can keep the conversation going for another five minutes, I'll capture Istar in a wall of Incarnation and then leave, I told myself.

"It's a play for time," said a faint voice in my arms.

With a start, I realized that behind the mask, Eolyne's eyes were narrowly open. He still seemed to be in pain, but his strength was coming back. That was a relief—but what did he mean by that?

He could sense my confusion and continued, "By now, they're evacuating personnel from the base down below. Once that's done, they're going to erase the facility itself."

"E-erase…? How…?" I gaped, looking down.

The view was blocked by thick clouds, but with a very delicate application of Incarnation, I could sense heat and movement. On the runway adjacent to the base, the large dragoncraft called an Avus was already running, with soldiers from the cargo bay rushing to load it up.

I had to be an idiot not to notice this activity. I thought I was being clever and getting information out of Istar, but I merely played myself right into their trap.

"…Very perceptive of you," said a cold voice up ahead, although it did contain a trace of emotion to it.

Eolyne, too, spit back at the mysterious figure with a notable change in emotion. "Just the sort of thing you would come up with, Tohkouga Istar."

"……!" I held my breath; they *knew* each other.

"I had a feeling you were our intruder, Eolyne Herlentz. Though you haven't gotten any sturdier, I see."

Eolyne seemed to frown at that comment. He looked to me and said, "I'm fine now. Let me down." At the end of his sentence, he mouthed, *Kirito*. I took that to be a message not to reveal my name.

I didn't have a problem with that strategy, but if I let him go, only insubstantial clouds awaited below. I'd have to create a foothold of Incarnation for Eolyne to stand on or keep a firm grip on him. He could see my obvious hesitation, and whispered, "You don't need to hold me up."

"...Got it," I said, and lowered my left arm, which had been propping Eolyne's legs up.

His black leather boots stood on nothing. Even after he hesitantly released my hand, the pilot commander's body did not suddenly plummet. In other words, Eolyne had mastered Incarnation flight just as well as Istar had.

Well, it had been two hundred years since the Otherworld War. Science had advanced to the point of flying to other planets, so it would stand to reason that similar advances and revolutions in Incarnate knowledge had happened, too. Naturally, that would include lessons in how to effectively master the art.

I had to tell myself that I could no longer think I was safe as long as I had Incarnate power.

The two stared each other down. Eolyne was the first to speak.

"Drop your gun and sword and surrender. What you are committing is undeniable rebellion against the Stellar Unification Council. I must apprehend you and take you to Centoria to be judged."

A faint smile grew on Istar's lips. "Still as uptight as you always were, Eol. If I were going to surrender just like that, I would've run away already and not chased you all the way up here."

"...You've changed, Kouga. The old you wouldn't have risked personal danger to buy time for subordinates to escape," Eolyne said.

This reminded me to check the surface below again. They were still loading the large dragoncraft; one could assume all the main facilities of the base were underground, so it would probably take time to transport things up the elevator. One of those things was presumably the device they used to turn the Divine Beast's children into bio-missiles. I really wanted to get the details on that. If the dragoncraft started up, I'd need to do something to stop it.

"Risk personal danger…?" Istar repeated, looking confused. They brushed windswept hair over their shoulder and continued, "I am doing no such thing, of course. I will simply occupy you until the Avus takes off, and after that I will walk…or fly…away."

Based on their tone of voice, Istar didn't expect any danger whatsoever. In their mind, there was no chance of them being apprehended, much less sustaining physical damage. Eolyne shrugged and said, "Yes, I take that back. You haven't changed. But it was that arrogance of yours that caused you to lose to me in the final of the Human Unification Tournament."

"A duel that forbids Incarnation is nothing more than a sideshow. I'm going to show you what a real battle looks like," Istar pronounced, and then drew their saber again in a long arc. A moment later, Eolyne pulled his sword from his belt.

Two swords shone crimson in the morning sun. While one was curved and the other was straight, their Object Class levels appeared equivalent. There was clearly some old score to settle between them, and I didn't really want to interfere in their fight, but I still had my Incarnate wall active, and if we weren't careful, the dragoncraft below was going to take off.

"Sorry, Eo, I'm gonna go ahead and execute a capture," I whispered, instantly changing the shape of the wall and ensnaring Istar in an invisible sphere.

There was no need to worry about the base alarm anymore, so I focused hard on strengthening the wall. Istar might be adept enough with Incarnation to fly, but I had blocked the Abyssal Horror's light rounds with this defensive wall. Istar's attacks wouldn't break through.

Istar floated forward within the invisible cage, extended a hand, and touched the wall.

It felt like something exceedingly cold slipped through my consciousness. The Incarnate wall wasn't broken, but Istar's hand passed right through it. It felt exactly the same as when the bio-missile had wriggled through the X'rphan's defensive shield—only dozens, hundreds of times stronger.

Incarnation-Eroding Incarnation.

Istar passed through the wall, cool as you please, and attacked Eolyne with ferocious speed.

21

Fortunately, there was no need to climb up the trunk of the massive tree in order to reach the entrance to the wasp nest, sixty feet off the ground. There was a large hollow in the roots of the tree, which formed a natural passageway inside the trunk traveling up to the nest.

After the death of the gilnaris queen hornet, the four soldier hornets and dozens of workers crumbled as one, and Chett's HP loss stopped, so there was no longer any concern. Still, Silica stood at the head of the insertion team and rushed up the passage, which was so tight that her shoulders nearly rubbed on either side.

The mossy passage made her shoes slip many times up the spiral tunnel, but at last she reached a large hollow space. There were hexagonal cells all over the walls, but any larvae or pupae had vanished along with the queen, so the cells were empty. She felt a tiny pang of pity, but more importantly...

"Chett! Where are you?!" Silica shouted, looking wildly all over the cave.

From the back, a faint voice replied, "I'm right here!"

Argo and Leafa caught up, and the three raced for the back wall, where they found a fresh tunnel. After crawling through,

they were in an even bigger cave. This was probably the center
of the nest because there were multiple exits on the left wall and a
raised platform on the opposite that looked like a throne.

And at its foot, stuck to the floor with what looked like gray
clay, was the tiny shape of a single Patter.

"Chett!"

Silica ran over and began to pull the sticky substance loose
with both hands. Once freed, Chett shook hard and leaped onto
her rescuer. "Thank you, thank you, Silica!"

"No, Chett...I'm sorry I wasn't able to get you free sooner. Are
you hurt?" she asked, then wondered if the NPCs in this world
even had the concept of "hurt."

But Chett's pointed snout wrinkled and shook side to side.
"The larvae just nibbled my tail a little. It's fine."

"Wh-what...?"

She glanced at Chett's tail, and sure enough, it was missing a
few inches off the end, and red damage effects were spilling from
the cut. But a missing part that small should return once her HP
was back to full.

Once she was calm again, Chett stepped away from Silica to
face the others. She beckoned to them and called out, "Come on,
everyone, over here!" and ran behind the throne.

Silica followed her and was dumbstruck when she saw what
was piled up back there.

Weapons, armor, accessories, items, and coins of gold, silver,
and bronze, glittered in the sunlight that shone through open-
ings in the nest.

The queen and her subordinates, unlike all the other monsters they'd fought to this point, immediately exploded and
dropped their resource items directly. As a matter of fact, the
man-faced centipede, the Life Harvester, had also worked
the same way, so perhaps the game considered it not worth the
trouble to need to dismantle a boss monster for parts. She'd simply assumed that the material rewards for defeating the gilnaris
queen hornet were wings, carapace, poison stinger, and the like.

"Oh, wowwww...There's so much treasure!" squealed Leafa.

Silica, however, was confused. "But...why would insect-type monsters be hoarding gold and weapons and valuables?"

"Ain't that obvious?" said Argo, picking up a coin and flipping it high into the air with her thumb. "When adventurers get captured and taken into the nest like Chett, they—"

"You don't need to spell it out!" Silica interrupted. Argo smugly caught the coin.

Indeed, there was no other way to interpret it. She felt bad about the idea of just looting it all, but if they didn't, either some other player was going to get it instead or it might be treated like abandoned items, which eventually lost durability until they crumbled away. Silica, Argo, and Leafa had charged into the nest first, so everyone else was waiting outside to find out what happened. They had to be quick.

"Do you think we can fit all of it into our inventory?" she asked, turning toward the others. Argo and Leafa grinned at her.

"Just about, I reckon."

"If we dump out all the logs first."

As soon as they saw Chett emerge from the hollow, the other Patter, Chinoki and Chilph, burst into excited chitters. The three hugged and pranced while the other human players, and even the Bashin warriors, looked on with pleased, relieved smiles.

But the mood changed when Silica, Argo, and Leafa dumped all the treasure they'd found onto the ground for everyone to see.

When fights started in MMORPGs, it was usually over fraud, insults, and item distribution. Silica had been adventuring with the same group since converting to *ALO*, but she'd teamed up with impromptu hunting parties all the time in *SAO*, and arguments had broken out more than a few times over loot. In fact, when she'd tried to get through the Forest of Wandering solo on the thirty-fifth floor, it was because one of her party members had said, "You don't need any healing crystals because that lizard will heal you already."

Of course, she might not have met Kirito if not for that experience, but when she thought back on her arrogance in that moment, it made her want to scream with embarrassment. Now she was determined to be fair and let the raid leader decide how the spoils should be distributed...

"We can figure that out once we get back to Ruis na Ríg," said Sinon, as cool as ever. That was enough to snap Klein and the others back to sanity from their state of giddy excitement over the mound of treasure. If they started talking about it now, they could be here for twenty or thirty minutes. The purpose of this whole exploration wasn't to defeat the wasp nest anyway, but to find a new spot for iron ore and to spot the path to the next step, as Friscoll had described it. They couldn't turn back yet.

First, they split the mass of treasure into multiple wooden chests, then sealed the lids with wax and gave them to strength-focused members. That way, if anyone tried secretly opening the contents while in their item window, the seal would be broken, and everyone would know.

Once the task was done, Silica took one last long look around the natural dome.

Through the branches of the massive tree that formed the canopy, the afternoon sunlight carved golden threads that hung in the air. The red-and-purple gargamol flowers were still in full bloom, but no hornets were coming to drink their nectar. The only remaining traces of the ferocious battle that had just taken place were the three bunkers near the tunnel, but almost all of them were out of durability and wouldn't be around much longer. Most likely the same fate would befall the nest stuck to the giant tree.

The place had been so full of the drone of giant hornet wings, but now the only sound was the rustling of the leaves in the gentle breeze. There was some undeniable guilt in Silica's mind over destroying an entire colony of living things, but the gilnaris hornets had also destroyed the Patter city in the past.

"Hey, let's go!" shouted Lisbeth.

Silica turned at the sound and saw all of her battle companions, packed and ready, smiling.

"Coming!" she cried, giving a signal to Misha (with Pina resting on the bear's head) before running back to join the others.

22

Even knowing it wasn't what I should be doing, I couldn't help but wait there and watch the aerial battle between Eolyne and Istar.

Unlike when I fought with Gabriel, there was no flashy, wild maneuvering here. If you ignored the fact that they were standing over nothing but a sea of clouds, it almost looked like an ordinary swordfight—except that all the attack and defense was augmented with Incarnation.

In other words, when guarding against the opponent's attack, if their mental image was even a fraction of a second late to bolster the sword, it would break. The same was true when attacking, too. No matter how fast you swung, if your imagination didn't keep pace with it, the other sword's block would cause your own to snap.

They were in an ultrafast exchange of blows, perfectly synchronizing and controlling their mental images at the same time. It was impossible without years of training. I certainly couldn't switch my Incarnation on and off this smoothly. It was an entire suite of Incarnate techniques; it made me want to call it the "Incarnation System."

And then, between the blinding exchange of blows between the two, there was a brief opening.

After a quick pause, Eolyne and Istar screamed together and erupted into high slashes like mirror images of each other.

"Haaaah!"

"Shieeea!"

Blade clashed with blade, creating a shock wave that seemed to flicker the very air itself. I could make out the tiniest little gap between the two swords, in fact. In that space was their Incarnation, each battling to destroy the other's sword.

The instant the pressure crossed its limits, the two were both knocked backward with a horribly grating metallic scrape.

The fight was even for now—but I was worried about Eolyne's strength, as he had been comatose just minutes earlier. Istar had mentioned something about Eolyne not being any sturdier. If they had known each other since childhood, then it would seem to confirm my fears that Eolyne was simply born with a weaker disposition.

In the mechamobile on the way to Central Cathedral, Eolyne had said that he won the Unification Tournament when he was sixteen. Going by their conversation, his opponent had been none other than Istar. That would make this, in fact, a duel between the greatest swordfighters in the Underworld to determine who truly stood at the pinnacle. It certainly didn't make me any more eager to interfere, but also, this was not a sporting competition. I had to step in and neutralize Istar when I saw the chance, before Eolyne ran out of strength.

My attempt at capturing via Incarnate wall was easily eroded, but there were plenty of other things I could do. If I shot a single heat element while they were locked together, it might distract Istar and allow Eolyne's slash to get through and destroy that saber.

I'll intercede on the next contact, I decided.

And just at that moment, several things happened at once.

First, two non-Avus dragoncraft took off from the runway below. They rose in a big arc, small and speedy. Probably fighters.

Next, the Avus began to proceed from the taxiway to the runway. They had finished loading the craft.

Also, deep underneath the base, a huge mass of heat and wind elements activated all at once.

The cloud of elements rapidly grew in pressure—and clearly not for energy supply purposes. As Eolyne hinted at, it was a means of eliminating the base—they were going to blow up that entire massive structure. But most horrifying of all, there were still over twenty staff members inside.

The fighters coming up from the right were probably backing Istar. Deal with them, prevent the Avus from taking off, and stop the base from exploding...There was absolutely no way I could do all these things on my own.

Eolyne and Istar opened space between them and readied their swords over their right shoulders. A yellow-green glow infused the blades—the cue for a sword skill.

There was only one thing I could do.

I pressed my thoughts into a supercharged, accelerated state. What was the highest priority? Supporting Eolyne, fighting off the attackers, blocking the Avus, or preventing the base explosion?

I thought I heard a voice.

I leave this to you now...Protect this...world...and its...people...

Words I'd heard long, long ago from the overseer and protector of the Underworld, the little sage Cardinal.

I kept those words close to my heart when I fought Administrator and Vecta. But the danger had not left this world yet. Since logging back in, I had been maintaining a kind of observational attitude, a distance between myself and the Underworld. But I had once fought for its sake, and the memories and feelings of the people who placed their hope in me before they left would never disappear. For the sake of Asuna and Alice, who put their trust in me when I left the cathedral, I had to do everything in my power.

Asuna...Alice...Cardinal.

Three faces passed through my mind, and in that instant, one single, absurd idea audibly clicked into place.

If Alice and Asuna were here right now, we could handle all these issues.

Of course, they were watching over Central Cathedral on Cardina, tens of thousands of miles away. It took an hour and a half for the X'rphan Mk. 13 to make the trip flying at Mach 300.

But with the sacred art of doors (teleport gates), which Cardinal had mastered, you could ignore physical distance. And really, the Underworld's version of "distance" wasn't even the same as actual space in real life.

I didn't know the sacred art formula to create a gate, of course, but Cardinal's old familiar, Charlotte, had told me that all sacred arts were merely tools for guiding and aligning Incarnation. As long as you imagined it hard enough, you could produce elements without speaking the command. Why not teleport gates?

I took my eyes off Eolyne and looked straight upward.

Cardina and Admina were rotating in the same direction at the same speed, but Cardina's Centoria and Admina's Ori were on opposite sides of their planets, meaning they were in a constant state of approaching and withdrawing. This was the time of day when Centoria and Ori were closest.

Just as Earth looked from the moon, the morning sky here contained a massive planet, half of it shining blue. My current location wasn't that far away from the city of Ori, so...

I saw it.

An artificial inverse triangle of a land mass. Red earth, with a brilliant green circle in the upper left, surrounded by white mountains. That was the human realm. In the middle was Centoria, and in the middle of *that* was Central Cathedral. I couldn't make it out with the naked eye, of course, but I could imagine it in my mind.

Using the spatial resources provided by the morning sun, I generated a vast amount of crystal elements and compressed them into place, into a single great door.

Underneath the translucent, crystalline door, I created a thin circular platform about twenty-five feet across. All this took one second...and in the next, I envisioned the figures of Asuna and Alice on that distant planet.

But they were not on that planet. They were just beyond the see-through door.

Distance does not exist here.

The morning light seen through the crystal door rippled like a disturbance in water.

On it appeared the vague image of two people wearing blue pilot uniforms I recognized—and just like that, I opened the door with my mind.

The pale, wavering image suddenly gained color and clarity. It was not a video. Through the crystal door, the fields of Admina and Central Cathedral on Cardina were connected.

"Asuna! Alice!" I bellowed for all I was worth, manipulating four kinds of Incarnation at once while the two were busy with some task. "Sorry! Help me out!"

If it were me in there, it would have taken ten seconds at bare minimum to recover from the shock, recognize the situation, judge that it was not a trap, and then go through the door.

But it took Asuna and Alice no more than half a second to react. They bolted into action without the slightest hint of doubt.

They came through the door one at a time, ran a few steps onto the clear platform, and stopped. There was nothing around but the dawning sky and the clouds below. That had to be a shock, for sure, but they didn't stop there.

"What should we do, Kirito?!"

"Asuna, make that entire base down below float into the air! There's a bomb underneath it that's about to explode!" I shouted, using a fifth line of Incarnation to sweep away an entire mass of clouds. It revealed the land below, where staffers were scrambling to evacuate the building, but there couldn't be more than ten seconds left until the blast.

Praying there wouldn't be any casualties, I gave my next order.

"Alice, stop that huge dragoncraft! Just don't destroy it entirely!"

The Avus was already accelerating down the runway. It was too late to stop it from taking off, but Alice would find a way to deal with it.

"You certainly do like to ask for the absurd!" the knight hissed, but drew the Osmanthus Blade from the left hip of her blue uniform.

"I'll find a way!" added Asuna. She was dressed the same way, but she did not draw Radiant Light, her pearly rapier. Instead, she lifted the large kitchen knife in her right hand.

Everything happened all at once.

Alice pointed the Osmanthus Blade straight ahead and shouted, "Enhance Armament!"

The Integrity Knight's secret art of Perfect Weapon Control activated, splitting the golden sword into a plethora of flower petals. They shone in the early sun, turning into a surge that shot downward to the surface.

Below, the Avus had just taken off from the runway. The flames of its engines, three under each wing, were long and red. It was rapidly gaining altitude.

From directly above, the flowers attacked, splitting into two streams that rushed after not the body or the engines but the flaps on the rear of the wings that controlled lift. The little mechanisms were gone without a trace.

There were no air molecules in the Underworld's atmosphere, but the dragoncraft flew on essentially the same logic as flight in the real world. Having lost the flaps, the wings didn't have enough lift and couldn't rise, but since the wings themselves were intact, the craft didn't just go into a nosedive.

The Avus unsteadily drifted back down and made an unplanned landing surrounded by yellow flowers. This time a swarm of *real* flower petals billowed up as it slid several hundred yards, then came to a stop at an angle.

Asuna pointed the knife in her hand toward the base and shouted, "Ready, set—!"

A rainbow of light touched down out of the sky and wreathed the massive structure.

There was a strange sound somewhat like a chorus of angels, and the gray building wrenched loose of the ground. The officers still in the process of evacuating jumped out in a panic, while others who didn't make it in time rushed back inside the building for safety.

Asuna's super-account for the goddess Stacia had powers of unlimited terrain manipulation. In the fight against the Abyssal Horror, she summoned a colossal meteor, and in the Otherworld War, she created a crack in the land several miles long. Lifting a single building was nothing compared to that.

Once the base had lifted off the ground in the rainbow aurora, I could see that the elongated basement portion made it look like a vertical rectangle. If the self-destruct mechanisms with the heat and wind elements were attached to the foundation, they'd need to be removed, but fortunately, they had been buried even deeper into the soil.

When it was entirely free, she announced, "There we go!" and slid the knife to the right. The building followed suit, and a few seconds later, a giant gout of flame belched up from the dark hole left behind in the earth.

The two craft that took off before the Avus continued their rapid ascent, seemingly unbothered by the instant whisking away of the clouds.

I could sense intuitively that the people sitting in the cockpits of the dragoncraft were Istar's personal servants, Sugin and Domhui.

They had a form factor similar to the Keynis Mk. 7, except that the color was a dark matte gray, with no insignia or numbers of any kind. The large cannons jutting from their undersides were already glowing with heat elements.

I'd handed over the task of stopping the Avus and preventing the base from being blown up to Alice and Asuna so I could control the fighters with Incarnation. But if I tried to grab them flying at that speed, it would cause them to crumble to pieces and possibly explode their sealed canisters. I didn't want any casualties if I could help it...and just like clockwork, they read my mind and opened fire on us.

The rapid-fire heated projectiles weren't aimed at me, nor were they aimed at Eolyne or the platform Alice and Asuna were standing on. They were focused on the black serpent, which was floating some distance away.

"Huh...?!" I yelped, and only barely intercepted in time. Nearly ten heat-element missiles collided with my Incarnate wall, creating a large orange explosion in the air.

Sugin and Domhui must have known that the Divine Beast was still unconscious. And they aimed at it anyway? Perhaps they had some strategic reason for needing to kill it, rather than letting it escape with its life.

In any case, I couldn't let them attack the Divine Beast.

I'm borrowing your sword, Eugeo, I thought, and pulled the Blue Rose Sword from my right side.

With the blue crystal tip pointed right at the dragoncraft, I shouted, "Enhance Armament!"

The sword took on a pure-blue shine, erupting with light that turned into ice thorns that twined and tangled as they bore down on the dragoncraft. The two craft quickly split left and right; the vines separated to follow as well. Just before making contact, they spread out like nets that caught and clung to the steel bodies.

The dragoncraft gunned their engines in the hopes of escaping the vines, but that didn't last for more than a second. With a heavy thud, a block of ice that came from seemingly nowhere enveloped the rear of the craft. It was growing bigger by the moment, until it had swallowed up the entire interior of the hefty fighter jets. Without their means of propulsion, the two craft fell toward the ground, spinning out of control.

The Blue Rose Sword's Perfect Weapon Control could wrap players in a big chunk of ice and neutralize them, as well as protect them. Nothing short of a truly extraordinary weapon or physical shock could break that ice. You'd need the same

priority level as the Blue Rose Sword to destroy it, or else use Incarnation.

The two flying icebergs dropped to the ground far below, bounced and tumbled violently, then came to a stop embedded in the slope of a tall hill. There wasn't a single crack in the ice, so the aircraft inside were totally unharmed. Sugin and Domhui probably got wickedly dizzy, but wouldn't have suffered much.

The Avus's crash landing, the explosion in the base's footprint, and the attack and crash of the fighters all happened at the same time.

But in their midst, Eolyne and Istar did not lose the slightest ounce of focus.

They held the Sonic Leap skill in their swords, waiting for the moment to arrive.

As I'd experienced many times before, when two combatants were evenly matched, it was often the case that you couldn't strike when facing off. The one who got impatient and moved first usually lost. Once in that situation, it was simply a battle of perseverance.

On top of that, they were both using Incarnation to stay still in the air. If this were *ALO*, they would be expending their flight gauge at every moment. Even the greatest Incarnate expert would eventually reach their limit, and in that sense, Eolyne was probably at a disadvantage because he had passed out after using Hollow Incarnation twice inside the base.

That was my reasoning for interfering with an elemental attack.

At the time I turned back after neutralizing the fighter craft, they were still at a standstill. Grateful that I was still in time, I held up my hand and made to generate a heat element that would distract Istar—when I felt someone gently hold back my hand.

It wasn't Asuna or Alice. They were still busy with wrapping up the Avus and base.

It wasn't Eolyne, either. All his attention was on Istar, and he likely didn't even see me.

Instead, my eyes dropped to the Blue Rose Sword in my left hand.

The blade, still in Perfect Control mode, sparkled with white particles like diamond dust.

Through the wavering haze, I thought...I saw someone's figure...

"Lord Eolyne!" someone shrieked, ripping through the dawn.

It was Stica. She was peering through the still-open crystal door, maple-red eyes wide.

Then the swordsmen moved.

They activated the Sonic Leap each had been holding and burst forward, leaving yellow lines behind them in the air, crossing the gap instantly, swinging saber and longsword.

There was a tremendous double ring of light and vibration that spread outward to rock the atmosphere.

Two sword skills, bolstered by Incarnation, each vying to crush the other. Power beyond limits was compressed into ultrafine bolts of purple lightning that surged repeatedly from the nexus point.

The standstill of immense power against power broke in a shocking way:

Eolyne's longsword and Istar's saber simultaneously crumbled to pieces.

They didn't cleave in two, but instead shattered into hundreds of tiny bits that sparkled and flew. The energy, now unleashed, caused a tremendous explosion, knocking back both combatants.

"Eolyne!"

I bolted forward and caught the pilot commander, propping him up with my right hand. There were a number of fine cuts on his chest and arms, but none seemed serious. He was also quite conscious still, and nodded that he was all right.

The remnants of light in the air soon faded, leaving only Istar floating twenty yards away.

Istar did not seem seriously hurt. But after the destruction of the saber, their Incarnation had to be heavily expended. There was still that gun, but it couldn't possibly have more power than the heat-element guns on the fighter craft.

We, on the other hand, had Asuna and Alice. Istar was undoubtedly powerful, but there was no way to even break free and escape from the three of us together, much less beat us all.

Eolyne straightened and stepped away from my arm, his feet firm on the air.

"I'll say it again. Surrender yourself, Kouga."

Istar's red lips curled into a faint smile. "I'm glad to see you haven't lost your touch, Eol." Then the smile vanished. They brushed the shards of metal from their coat. "But you're still just as naïve. You won't beat me unless you can overcome."

Their hand a blur, Istar moved swiftly to pull out the black pistol.

I wasted no time in deploying an Incarnate wall in the midpoint between them. Istar could slip through the wall in person, but surely a bullet wouldn't have the same power. Let them fire all their bullets first, and then I could physically apprehend them...

But Istar instead pointed the gun straight upward and, to my shock, said, "Enhance Armament."

With a loud clank, the black gun changed shape and emitted crimson light from the cracks.

Perfect Weapon Control.

Meaning Istar's main weapon wasn't the shattered saber, but the gun...

Red light poured from the muzzle when the trigger was pulled, penetrating the wall of Incarnation and spreading in a spherical shape.

There was no heat or pain when the light passed through me. Instead, I was assaulted by the unpleasant sensation of cold hands caressing my soul.

Immediately, I was reminded of when Mutasina's suffocation magic affected me in *Unital Ring*. The effect itself was completely different, but there was a similarity in their menacing, curse-like nature. What was the effect of this—?

The answer came before I could finish wondering the question.

First, the crystal door I generated vanished, along with Stica's face peering through from the other side.

Asuna and Alice screamed and began to fall. I tried to lift them back up with Incarnation, but at this point Eolyne and I were falling, too.

No matter how hard I demanded it, the drop would not reverse itself. My imagination was being canceled out, just before it could overwrite the rules of the world.

An Incarnation-nullification zone. That was the nature of Istar's Perfect Weapon Control.

But then Istar shouldn't be able to fly, either. I looked up, searching, and found a black shape plummeting elsewhere and moving fast. Istar's arms were pressed flat to their body in a skydiver's pose, intentionally adding speed.

Their destination was the two dragoncraft that had crashed on the hill to the north. Because of the Release Recollection art, the ice had already melted, and both craft were opening their canopies. Was Istar going to take Sugin and Domhui and then escape? But if they hit the ground at that speed, even Istar wasn't going to survive.

The answer was actually much simpler than that.

Just before Istar would have slammed into the ground, they used wind elements rather than Incarnation, generating and bursting them to create a blast of air to cushion the fall and land safe and sound.

After a quick spin, Istar took off running toward one of the pilots tumbling out of their dragoncraft—I guessed it was Domhui—grabbed his arm and rushed toward the other craft. Once Sugin was up on his feet, Istar pulled both of them up the hill.

For a brief moment, Istar turned back to watch Eolyne fall. But it was so far away that I couldn't make out any expression on that beautiful face.

The three of them crossed the line of the hill and went out of sight.

Then the two dragoncraft promptly exploded. Sugin and Domhui must have activated a self-destruct mechanism. The Incarnation-nullifying bubble ended at the top of that hill. Once there, Istar could resume Incarnation flight. Unfortunately, we didn't seem to have any means to prevent their escape.

The bigger problem was our continued plummet toward the ground. Asuna and Alice weren't screaming anymore, but they *were* looking at me expectantly, thinking, *What now?* Since I couldn't use Incarnation here, I'd have to keep falling and cancel out the impact the same way Istar had.

I was just about to tell the others to prepare some wind elements—when a long, black, tubular object came soaring upward from below and caught me and Eolyne. The tube continued toward the girls and picked them up, too.

At five feet across and at least sixty feet long, the flying object was none other than the black serpent kept captive inside the base—the Divine Beast. At some point, it had awakened from its coma, flown through the Incarnation-nullification zone, and come to save us.

On the end of the snake in the direction we were moving was a slight bulge for the head. A tiny black snake was stuck to the top, its tail wriggling energetically.

The Divine Beast descended close to the ground before floating upward again. That was when I noticed the crew of the crashed Avus and the other base staffers who had escaped the explosion watching us in amazement.

"...Eo, what should we do about them?" I asked.

The pilot commander shrugged. "We'll have to leave them here for now. As long as we've got the large dragoncraft and the base itself, we have plenty of evidence of their conspiracy."

"Good point..."

About ten feet behind us were Asuna and Alice. They were still having difficulty grasping the situation. I walked carefully along the smooth scales of the Divine Beast's back to approach them.

Asuna asked, "Kirito, what is this giant snake?"

"It's apparently a Divine Beast that's been living on Admina."

"Divine Beast?!" shouted Alice. Her blue eyes sparkled, and she knelt down to caress the scales. "I've never seen a living Divine Beast before. Uh…if you don't count the Abyssal Horror, that is."

"That probably doesn't count." I chuckled. Then I straightened up and bowed to the girls. "Alice, Asuna, thank you for helping us. It would have been pretty bad if you weren't there."

"You're entirely welcome, of course, but that door—," Asuna started to say.

But she was cut off by a sonorous, echoing woman's voice inside my head.

"Dark King, where wouldst thou have me take thee?"

"Wh-what?!"

I looked around for the source of the voice. Belatedly, I realized that it belonged to the Divine Beast.

The base was now far behind us, and we had left the nullification area. We could fly with Incarnation at this point, but I wasn't opposed to getting a ride.

"W-wait a minute!" I shouted in the direction of the beast's head, then deployed some Incarnate radio waves in the direction I was guessing. The response was immediate, so I pointed ahead and to the left. "Fly us over there!"

"Over there" was a very vague order, but the Divine Beast changed direction at once. We flew over yellow flower fields for several minutes until a very small hill appeared. Without even needing the order from me, the serpent rose to the top of the hill and came to a gentle landing.

The four of us hopped off its back and turned around a short distance away. The Divine Beast's massive length coiled into a pyramidal mound, and it looked down at us with three eyes.

"Thou hast my gratitude for freeing me and my child from that prison, Dark King," said the ringing voice in my head. The child was surely the little black snake now riding on the Divine Beast's head.

Istar's group had forced the Divine Beast to give birth, then turned the children into bio-missiles. I couldn't have guessed how many had been victimized this way until I got here, and I didn't want to ask.

"Uh...we're the ones who should be thanking you. Humans like us inflicted those terrible things on you, but you saved our lives anyway. Thank you."

Asuna, Alice, and Eolyne joined me in bowing.

"I am well aware that thy kind contains both the virtuous and the wicked. Those who captured me will one day pay the price for their deeds."

"We'd be glad to help," I offered, raising my head. I got the impression that the Divine Beast *smiled* somehow.

From the rear of the giant coil, the pointed tip of its tail came reaching over to me. A leather bag was tied to the tip with string.

"Take this."

"Huh? Wh-what is it...?"

"Thou gavest it to me thyself, many seasons ago. Thou saidst that when thee returned after time's passage, I should relinquish it to thee."

"......!"

I held my breath. If this was true, then when I was the Star King, I had left something behind in the anticipation that I would one day return to the Underworld.

"I was meant to gift it after thee had crossed the planet hither and thither, completing numerous ordeals...but having found ourselves in each other's company this way, I cannot begrudge thee this early bequeathing. Take it."

The tail stretched out farther, so I grabbed the bag with both hands.

The tip of the tail slipped out of the rope knot and returned to the coil. If I were to interpret the Divine Beast's words, it seemed His Majesty the Star King had left something of an epic questline for me to complete, at the end of which I was meant to encounter the Divine Beast. But Istar captured the beast, and I had just rescued it, so the quest was all for nothing. A part of me was disappointed, I would admit, but the part that thought I had just lucked out was ten times as big.

"*Until we meet again, Dark King...White Queen, Golden Knight, and Blue Swordsman,*" the Divine Beast announced. The baby snake atop its head added a spunky hiss for good measure.

The pitch-black serpent lifted its long body and curled upward into the sky. When it had reached a distant height, it shot off toward the sun with tremendous speed.

No one said anything for several moments. It was Alice who eventually broke the silence.

"...What is that, Kirito?"

"Oh, this. I think it's..."

I undid the rope around the mouth of the bag and reached inside. What I pulled out was a box about eight inches to a side, made of some mysterious material that seemed like it could be either glass or metal. There was nothing written on the outside, but I was certain I knew what it contained.

"This is the sealed chest, Alice. Everything about the Deep Freeze art is contained in here."

"Wha...?!"

She put her hands over her mouth. Her sapphire-blue eyes were full of rainbow color.

23

4:27 PM, October 3rd, 2026 (December 7th, Stellar Year 582).

Asuna, Alice, Eolyne, and I returned to Central Cathedral on Cardina, along with the X'rphan Mk. 13.

Of course, we did not force the damaged X'rphan to fly. I created another portal door, this one massive, right next to the immobile craft, then lifted it with Incarnation and somehow managed to push it through.

For now, I couldn't connect the door to coordinates unless Asuna or Alice was there, or it was a place I'd been before and could easily imagine. The problem was that when I opened the first door, the girls were not on the Morning Star Lookout, but the kitchen on the ninety-fourth floor.

Naturally, the second door also connected to the kitchen, so Asuna and Alice jumped through, then traveled to the ninety-fifth floor while I waited on Admina. Then I created the door again to their current coordinates, where it was safe to put the aircraft. In gaming terms, it was like setting up my fast travel locations to the first and second floor of the same building, but that wasn't going to be a problem for the time being.

I passed through the door with the X'rphan the second time, putting me and Eolyne on the ninety-fifth floor. Naturally, we were bombarded with questions by Stica and Laurannei.

As it happened, Stica had peered through the portal when coming to pick up the food and witnessed the conclusion of the fight between Eolyne and Istar. Naturally, she was dying to know what had happened, and while I wanted to explain it to her, I would use up all the valuable time remaining if I responded to every question.

So I forced the pilot commander to be our answer sheet while Alice, Asuna, and I rushed down the great stairs to the Cloudtop Garden on the eightieth floor.

Alice clutched the sealed chest tightly and barely waited for the double doors to open before bursting into the garden. She flew up the green hill.

At the top, caressed by the osmanthus tree, one girl and two knights waited in eternal slumber under the effect of the forbidden Deep Freeze art, which Administrator had concocted generations ago...

Alice knelt before her beloved sister, Selka, and placed the bluish-gray box on the grass. Asuna and I, and Eolyne, Stica, Laurannei, and Airy with her friend Natsu all watched with bated breath.

She ran her fingers along the sides of the chest and lifted. The lid, which had been so close to the box that it seemed there was no seam at all, came loose, revealing the box's contents.

The interior was lined with deep-blue velvet. There were a number of depressions in the surface, holding a small scroll and three crystal bottles. Alice looked back to me with confusion.

"I think the scroll has the entire formula for Deep Freeze on it," I explained, "and the bottles contain a solution that corresponds to the formula that undoes it."

"Solution...? So we don't need to chant the entire formula? We just sprinkle the contents of the bottle, and it will undo the petrification?"

I nodded.

Alice faced the box again and reached down to pull out the bottle on the right.

It had a multifaceted surface, like a cut gem. She stared at it for a moment, then crawled closer to Selka on her knees. She pressed a hand to her chest, breathing heavily, then pulled the top off the bottle.

If this doesn't do the trick, Star King, I'm gonna sock you in the mouth, I thought to my past self, waiting for the moment to arrive.

Alice reached out.

Her hand rotated slowly, trembling, until the bottle was past level over Selka's head.

The liquid that poured from the narrow mouth of the bottle shone blue in the light, as though it were glowing all on its own. It dripped over Selka's bangs, down her cheeks, and gathered to drip off the underside of her chin.

One...two...three...

Five seconds felt like an eternity, but then it was over.

Blue light gently enveloped Selka's frozen body.

Her toes and fingers, robe hem, and other extremities gradually began to regain their original color and texture. The osmanthus tree behind her began to rustle, as though understanding the importance of what was happening here.

The veil of white on Selka's head began to sway in the breeze.

A lock of bright-brown hair fell over her forehead.

Her eyelashes trembled, slowly rising...

Indigo-blue eyes, bleary and dull, looked upon the world, then blinked and blinked again, gaining focus. Her pink lips moved, then uttered a faint but undeniable sound.

"………Alice…?"

"Selka!!"

Alice toppled onto her sister, her voice wet with tears already. She pressed her face into the shoulder of the white robe, circled her arms around Selka's back, and called her name over and over.

Tears ran down Selka's cheeks, too. "Alice, oh, Alice!" she repeated.

I had to rub my forearm across my eyes. I approached the box,

which was now sitting behind Alice, crouched down to pick up the other two bottles, and handed one to Asuna.

"Go ahead and pour this on Tiese."

"Okay!"

Asuna was blinking back tears but smiling, too.

I walked to Selka's right and pulled out the stopper in front of Ronie.

She looked about ten years older than when she'd been my page. She had grown taller, but her face was absolutely the same.

I'm back, I whispered silently, and poured the vial over her head. The same exact process occurred here, starting at the end of her robe and rising, turning her from stone to living before my eyes.

Her neck, cheeks, and then eyes regained signs of life. Her bangs rustled in the breeze. Her eyelids fluttered...and then opened.

Eyes the color of a clear lake stared right into mine.

That was when I recalled what Airy had said: Ronie and Tiese underwent life-freezing arts in their mid-twenties and spent another fifty years before they were petrified here. Meaning their mental age was over seventy now. Compared to them, I was nothing but a sassy little kid...

But my fears were totally unfounded.

"...Kirito!!"

Her voice and expression were exactly as I remembered them from Swordcraft Academy. Ronie leaped forward and hugged me. I awkwardly returned the gesture and patted her back.

"It's been a while, Ronie. I'm glad to see you again," I managed to stammer.

She squeezed me even harder and repeated, "Yes...yes!"

After a good five seconds of that, her mind finally caught up to the situation, and she cried, "Oh...what about Tiese and Selka?!"

"They're fine. We've unfrozen both of them, too," I said, pulling away.

But when I turned around, I was met with a sight I had not expected.

Tiese, having been brought back to life by Asuna's application of the solution, had taken a few steps forward. Her red eyes were open wide, staring.

Staring at the face of Integrity Pilot Commander Eolyne Herlentz, covered by his white mask...

(To be continued)

AFTERWORD

Thank you for reading *Sword Art Online 26: Unital Ring V.*

The Unital Ring arc started at the end of 2018, and now we're at the fifth volume, and it's about time for the story of these two worlds to really begin heating up toward a climax...but I keep finding more things I need to write and things I want to write, and I put myself in the difficult position of having to choose what to include or not. Not that that's any different from usual!

(Spoilers for this volume to follow.)

Even still, I managed to reach a major milestone I had my eyes on from the start of the UR arc: the revival of Ronie, Tiese, and Selka, which I felt very emotional about. Every time I mentioned that it had been two hundred years since the Underworld and Moon Cradle arcs, I myself had to wonder, "Will we *really* see those three again...?" Thankfully, we managed to get to Admina and retrieve the formula for the Deep Freeze art within this volume. I was just as relieved as Kirito was about that.

Of course, this isn't happily ever after. I ended off with "to be continued" right as you wonder what will happen to Tiese when she sees Commander Eolyne right after waking up! I think we'll be finding out more about the commander's mysteries next time, so look forward to it!

Meanwhile, the conquest of *Unital Ring* continues, including a look at the shape of the overall world this time. I hope you enjoyed seeing Silica and Sinon hold their own against a supertough field boss in Kirito and Asuna's absence, and got a feel for how much they've grown.

Now, in October 2021, when this book comes out in Japan, the movie *Sword Art Online Progressive: Aria of a Starless Night* is about to hit theaters!

This one is an exciting gamble, a retelling of the story of Aincrad, where it all began, from Asuna's perspective. As the author, and a fan of Kirito and Asuna, I'm really looking forward to seeing this on the big screen. I would be really delighted if you all show up at the theater!

We had a lot of trouble after the initial submission of the text this time, and I'm very, very sorry to our illustrator, abec, and editors, Miki and Adachi, for that. I'll do my best to make things smoother next time! Thank you all for reading!

Reki Kawahara—September 2021